somewhere else

SANDRA GLOVER

somewhere else

ANDERSEN PRESS LONDON

First published in 2008 by
Andersen Press Limited,
20 Vauxhall Bridge Road, London SW1V 2SA
www.andersenpress.co.uk
www.sandraglover.co.uk

British Library Cataloguing in Publication Data available

ISBN 978 184 270 815 6

Typeset by FiSH Books, Enfield, Middx
Printed and bound in Great Britain by
CPI Bookmarque, Croydon, CR0 4TD

1

Tell them. Have to get back.

Her eyes snapped open. Strange, she was already back, in bed, in her room. So had she already told them? But no, the room was all wrong. It wasn't *her* room. Dreaming, that was it, she was dreaming. Close eyes – open them again, slowly this time. Sit up.

No! What was going on? Where was she? This was all wrong.

A fleeting memory of her real room: flowery wallpaper, dark brown wardrobe, dressing table – not much space for anything else. Then this room, imprinting on her senses, overwhelming her. Long, huge narrow room painted pale yellow. Low white ceiling with wooden beams. Attic! It was an attic. Funny furniture perfectly fitted into the irregular shapes of the room. Posters on the walls. Not her posters. Clothes on the floor. Not her clothes. She threw off the bedclothes, which felt all wrong, from a bed that felt wrong. She got up and moved towards the door.

Awake, she was definitely awake – so was the other place a dream? But where was she now, who was she? She couldn't remember. She could remember the names of things, objects, or at least some of them, but not her own name. She couldn't remember her name or anything about herself. Her body felt strangely light but clumsy, somehow. Ill, was she ill? Her head was hazy, like a mist was swirling inside it, making it impossible to think, to focus. There were images, memories maybe, faces, places caught up in the mist but nothing clear, nothing she could hold on to.

She opened the door and saw another door opposite. It was closed. There was a sign in large green letters. 'ZAN. KEEP OUT.' What was a ZAN? Shivering slightly, she tried to pull the short, long-sleeved nightdress she was wearing down a bit before moving on towards the stairs.

Blue carpet, soft, furry, tickling her bare feet. At the bottom of the stairs there was a hall with more doors, more blue carpet leading to another flight of stairs. Whose house was she in? It was big, far too big to be hers, or at least that's how it felt but she couldn't be sure.

There were sounds coming from downstairs; voices and clattering. Who was it? Who lived here? She walked down the second flight, heart beating too fast, chest tight. At the bottom of the stairs was a slightly bigger hall with paintings on the wall and a large mirror. Someone was standing there, by an open door; a boy, looking at her. A short cry escaped before she could stop it.

'Hey,' said the boy. 'What's wrong? Why're you lookin' at me like that?'

He was skinny, tallish, about fourteen, she guessed. Younger than her maybe though she wasn't sure how old she was. The boy was wearing a uniform, a school uniform. Ordinary, nothing odd about him except she didn't know him, hadn't ever seen him before.

'Who are you?' she asked.

'Duh!' said the boy. 'Zan. Same as always. Zan. Zander. Alexander. Your brother?' he said, emphasising each word.

'I haven't got a brother.'

She knew that. She didn't know how she knew but she did. Sisters, she had older sisters, two of them. Names, what were their names?

'You wish!' the boy was saying. 'Hey Jade, what is it, what's wrong? Nightmares again, a migraine? Come on! Stop looking at me like that, you're spooking me.'

She looked round to see who he was talking to. There was no one there.

'Jade?' he said. 'Are you OK? You look – I dunno – your eyes are all sort of weird.'

Jade. He kept saying Jade. Was he talking to her, was she Jade? The name seemed sort of familiar but no – the answer came to her in an instant.

'I'm Janet,' she said. 'I'm Janet. I don't live here. I don't know how I got here.'

'Mum,' the boy called. 'Mum! There's somethin' wrong with Jade again.'

He said 'again' as though this had happened before! A woman appeared but it wasn't Mum. This wasn't Mum. Slim, short hair, gingery-blonde like Zan's. Black trousers. Black and white top. Short sleeves. Slightly tanned arms. Thin face, longish nose, anxious eyes.

'You look tired, love,' the mum-person said. 'Head-ache?'

Janet shook her head, trying not to cry out. What was happening, what was going on? She pushed past them towards the mirror. This time she couldn't stop herself. She screamed. Not a short scream but one that went on and on, gaining its own momentum as she stared at the mirror. This wasn't her, it couldn't be! The light blonde hair, mid-length, cut all sort of jagged and the eyes, very green, very bright. Too bright, feverish almost, manic, scary, looking huge in a pale, thin face. And that scar on her cheek – what was that doing there? She shouldn't have a scar. She stared at the nightdress, the long legs. How was she supposed to look, why did it feel so wrong?

'Jade,' the woman was saying. 'Come on, come and sit down. You've had another nightmare, yes?'

Nightmare, was that all it was, that other place she'd been in? It hadn't felt like a nightmare though; a dream perhaps, a nice dream, but definitely not a nightmare. She couldn't quite remember it but it had felt right, somehow – safe.

Hands on her shoulders now, steering her, guiding her into a room with glass doors looking out onto a long garden. The woman making her sit down on a beige settee that she'd never sat on before, didn't recognise, just like she didn't recognise anything else about the room. Television in the corner but it looked odd, not quite like a real television.

'OK, that's better,' the woman said as Janet sat back quietly sobbing. 'You're all right now.'

'She didn't recognise me,' Zan was muttering. 'I don't think she recognised herself.'

'Don't be daft,' Mum said. 'Of course she did. She's just upset, confused. The nightmares – it'll pass in a minute. You recognise us now, don't you, Jade?'

Jade, why did they keep calling her that? It felt familiar, as if she might know someone called Jade but it wasn't her, it couldn't be her. She shook her head and tried to push the woman away.

'She says she's not Jade,' Zan began. 'She says she's Janet. I mean, what's all that about? D'yer reckon it's . . . '

'Stress,' his mum snapped, talking hurriedly, nervously all the time. 'I told you it's just the nightmares. She'll be fine in a minute or two. You'd better get off to school, Zan.'

'Yeah, right,' said Zan, 'and leave her on her own, like this?'

'She won't be on her own. I'll phone work if she doesn't get any better, tell them I won't be in, again.'

'I can stay,' said Zan.

'No, you can't. You're going to school.'

'There's only two days left! There's no point. Why don't you let me stay with her, while you go to work? You can't keep taking time off and we're not doing nothing at school.'

'According to your teachers, you never do anything, that's the problem! Now just go, Zan. I've got enough to worry about, without you kicking off.'

'I'm not kicking off. I'm just trying to help.'

Janet looked from the boy to the woman as they argued. It felt as though she'd heard all this before but she couldn't have done. She didn't know these people, she couldn't stay here. She had to get home, tell them something, but what? Where was home? What did she have to tell them? Why couldn't she remember, why was she so tired? Why was it so hard to move? Why was she so mixed-up, confused?

'I want my mum,' she sobbed. 'I want my mum.'

'I'm here,' said the woman.

'Not you! I want Mum.'

A picture, so brief it was barely there at all before it was gone. Mum in the small kitchen at home. Mum with her dark hair, wavy, slightly messy. Then this new place, these new people, taking over, pushing the memories away.

'Leave me alone! Let me go!'

Those words, she recognised them, she'd said them before! She felt suddenly sick, pressure inside her head building as if the mistiness had turned to thick black fog, creeping over her brain, smothering it, shutting it down not letting her remember.

'Zan, get her tablets before you go,' the woman told the boy who was hovering by the door.

'Do you think we should?' he asked. 'It might be the tablets making her like this.'

'Don't be stupid, Zan,' his mum said. 'It's got nothing to do with the tablets. God knows what she'd be like without them! But bring my phone as well, will you? I think I'll get the doctor to check her over.'

The words sounded distant, as though they were floating round the room so it was hard to catch them and even harder to form her own words.

'I don't need a doctor,' she managed to say. 'I just want to go home!'

'Where's home then?' said Zan, quietly, coming towards her.

'Don't,' his mum snapped. 'Don't encourage – whatever it is. Just get the phone and the tablets.'

'I don't know,' Janet said, blinking, trying to clear away the fog. 'I can't remember. I can see it, sometimes, well bits of it. Not clearly. It's hazy like a dream.'

'That's it,' said the woman, gently, 'that's what I'm

trying to tell you. It was just a dream, Jade. This is home, this is where you live. You've lived here all your life.'

'No! Not here,' Janet insisted.

It couldn't be here, she didn't want it to be here. She wanted to go back – somewhere.

'Somewhere different,' she said. 'Somewhere else.'

Wrong doctor. Wrong surgery. She'd never been here before, never met this man, this Dr Carr, although he seemed to know her, or know Jade. Janet gripped the edge of her chair, wanting to hold onto something, anything solid, while the mum-lady talked.

'It just came on, suddenly, this morning,' the woman was saying. 'It's not quite like the other times, the nightmares. I mean, there's been days, well most days I suppose, when she's woken up totally confused, disorientated, anxious, but it's only lasted an hour or so. Nothing like this! She doesn't seem to know anybody, anything. Couldn't find the bathroom, couldn't find her way out of the house. She cried all the way here.'

Dr Carr nodded, pushing his oval glasses further up his slightly crooked nose.

'All right,' he said, swinging his chair round slightly. 'I just want to take your temperature first, Jade, OK? There's nothing to worry about. I won't hurt you. What are you looking at?' he added, smiling at her, his teeth amazingly straight and white.

'That,' said Janet.

The thing he'd been tapping at ever since they'd come in, watching a screen as he tapped. Something she half-recognised but couldn't name.

'The keyboard,' he said, sounding slightly troubled, slightly amused. 'The computer?'

'She's been like this all morning,' the mum-woman said. 'It's not like total amnesia. She remembers some things but not others. She can still read. She was reading magazines in the waiting room but she was asking questions about some of the people, some of the celebrities. Stuff she should know.'

On and on she went, telling him everything that had happened; every detail of every conversation.

'Zan thinks it might be the tablets,' she finished.

'I don't think so,' said Dr Carr. 'It's much more likely to be . . .'

He paused, nodded at the mum-person, like they were sharing a secret.

'What?' Janet said. 'What is it, what's wrong with me? How can I be two people? How can I be Jade and Janet?'

'You're not,' said Dr Carr, smiling at her again, stretching out, lightly touching her hand with his cold fingers. 'There's only one of you, I promise! It's just that sometimes, after a major trauma, the brain can do strange things, close off a bit of itself.'

'Trauma?' she asked, as a shadow of a memory

surfaced. 'Accident, I had an accident, yes?'

'Sort of,' said Dr Carr. 'I guess you don't remember any, er, details?'

'No, I don't know, I'm not sure. Something happened. I've got scars,' she said, touching her cheek. 'On my arms and – other places,' she added, shivering at the memory of what she'd seen earlier when she was getting dressed. 'But I don't know how I got them. I don't know what happened.'

She didn't really want to know. She could feel the shivering getting more intense, the fog in her head thickening, her limbs getting heavier, everything shutting off.

'That's all right,' said Dr Carr, looking at her, then at the mum-lady again. 'Maybe you don't want to remember. And maybe that's best, for now.'

Was he reading her mind? No, it was lies, illusions, tricks. They were all in on it somehow. Zan, the woman, the doctor, all trying to trick her, make her believe she was Jade, make out she was going mad. But why, who were they, why would they do that? How had they changed everything? Even the way she looked! Had they hurt her, had *they* caused the scars, messed with her body, her mind? She didn't think so but she couldn't be sure. Why couldn't she remember? Almost without realising, she stood up and headed for the door.

'Jade, love,' the woman said, standing up, blocking her path, 'what are you doing, where are you going?'

'Home.'

'I think it might be best if we get Jade back to hospital for a couple of days, Mrs Wallace,' said the doctor. 'Run some more tests.'

Wallace. Janet played with the name, rolling it over in her mind. Wallace, Jade Wallace. Wrong!

'You can't trick me,' she told the woman. 'I know. I know who I am. I'm Janet. Janet Bailey. And I'm not going to hospital. I'm going home. I have to get home.'

'Wait! Jade, Janet,' said the doctor as Janet tried to lurch towards the door. 'Listen, how would it be, if you stayed with Mrs Wallace and her family for a while, just until we find out a few things, eh?'

Did he think she was stupid, that she hadn't noticed him wink at the woman? Fine, let them think they'd got her, let them think they'd won. Until she could work it out, work out exactly who she was and how to get home.

'All right,' she said, sitting down again, 'but I don't have to go to hospital?'

'No,' said the woman, as though she was fighting back tears, 'you don't have to do anything you don't want to do.'

'We'll increase the tablets, a bit,' said the doctor. 'She's already on quite a high dose but it won't do any harm, just for a week or two. And I'll make you an appointment at outpatients to get some more tests done, in case it's anything physical, though I doubt it. There's also a, er,

11

specialist I'd like you to see, a Dr Mitchell. She's very good. Meanwhile,' he added, turning to the mum-person, 'make sure Jade gets lots of rest.'

'She has been,' Mum said. 'She's done nothing but sleep since the exams finished. But it's restless sleep, feverish, dreaming all the time.'

'Exams,' said Janet, clutching onto the word, holding it in her head. 'I remember doing exams.'

Important exams, exams she had to pass. School hall, rows of desks, teacher prowling, clock ticking, arm aching, brain bursting with facts she had to spew out.

'Good,' said Dr Carr, 'that's good. You'll probably find things will slowly start to come back. You'll see. I'm sure this is only temporary, I'm sure you'll be fine again in a day or two – maybe even sooner.'

He paused, smiling at her again. He was always smiling. He smiled too much.

'I'm going to ask our nurse to show you a few breathing and relaxation techniques that might help you, while I have a little chat to your mum, to Mrs Wallace, all right?'

Breathing! As if that would help! She knew how to breathe. It was the things she didn't know that were the problem. Like who she really was and what she was doing here.

2

Zan burst into the kitchen, throwing his bag across the floor.

'Boooring!' he said. 'Waste of time, I knew it would be. Watched a DVD, played a stupid game in maths and tidied cupboards. Got any biscuits? I'm starving! How is she, how's Jade?'

'She's asleep at the moment,' Mum said, 'on the settee, in the lounge. She's spark out, has been for about an hour.'

'So is she any better?' Zan asked, rummaging in the biscuit tin.

'Three's enough,' his mother said, tapping his hand as he reached for a fourth biscuit. 'And no, she isn't. If anything, she's worse. She's barely moved, hasn't eaten anything again. She's lost so much weight I'm not surprised she doesn't recognise herself! Anyway I did one of those little quiches for lunch. You know – the ones she loves – but she wouldn't touch it. She looked at it like she'd never seen a mini-quiche before. Then when I mentioned it was her favourite, from Marks & Spencer's, she kicked off.'

'What about?' said Zan crunching a ginger-nut.

'M&S of all things,' said Mum. 'She said she'd been there once, with her mum!'

'Yeah, well, you do go there a lot. More or less live there most Saturdays.'

'Exactly, she said once not every week! She wasn't talking about me, Zan. She was talking about this other mother she's dreamt up. Apparently her proper mum doesn't think much to M&S, says it's too expensive for the likes of them. I mean, where's she got that from?'

'Dunno but at least Jade's remembered the shop. At least she's remembered something,' Zan said, crunching his second biscuit.

'Can't you eat that quietly?'

'Sorry.'

'No, *I'm* sorry,' said Mum. 'I'm completely strung out. I can't seem to help her, get through to her. She won't let me hug her, squirms if I touch her.'

'Yeah, well that's been going on for a while, since . . . '

'I know but it doesn't make it any easier!'

'So did you get to the doctor's?' Zan asked.

'Yes and he's convinced it's all to do with . . . what happened.'

Zan stared at his mother. That's how they always

14

talked about it, if they mentioned it openly at all. Vague. 'What happened'. Never naming it, never saying the words! Because you couldn't, because even thinking about it ripped your guts out. And if it was like that for them, what was it like for Jade? No wonder she was trying to hide away in some freaky dream world.

'He reckons,' Mum was saying, 'that it's a form of post-traumatic stress.'

'Like soldiers get?'

'It's not just soldiers,' Mum said. 'It can be triggered by anything, any sort of dreadful experience. And there are degrees. Sometimes it's mild, short-lived, sometimes much deeper. Sometimes it doesn't kick in until months or, occasionally, even years after the event. Anyway Dr Carr's not an expert but he thinks Jade's created this fantasy world because she doesn't want to cope with the real one.'

'Yeah, well, can you blame her?' said Zan, slowly. 'But she seemed to cope OK at first, sort of. Didn't she? I mean, with the help of the tablets...'

'Too well,' said Mum. 'Dr Carr thinks that's part of the problem. The way she just threw herself into revision the minute she came out of hospital, insisted on doing her exams, like nothing had happened!'

'Not quite!'

'No, not quite but you know what I mean. While she was focused on her work, it was an escape, of sorts.

15

Now it's all finished, Dr Carr reckons it's surfaced again, big time. It's delayed reaction. That's why the nightmares have been getting worse. And now this complete...'

Breakdown. Mum stopped short of saying the word but Zan knew what she meant.

'Anyway,' Mum added, 'he wants her to see a Dr Mitchell, a psychologist.'

'What did Jade say?'

'Nothing much, we haven't told her it's a psychologist, not yet.'

And when they did? Zan didn't think she'd go for it just like she'd refused to see a trauma counsellor. It was probably a mistake. She should have seen someone, at the time, but no way could they persuade her. And they could hardly force her, could they?

'I don't need some bloody stranger prying,' she'd screamed at the policewoman who'd first mentioned it. 'Don't you think it's bad enough without having to tell anyone else about it! It's over now, finished. I just want to forget it, OK?'

But you couldn't, could you? You couldn't ever completely forget something like that. Or maybe you could. Maybe that was what Jade was doing, losing the memories, losing her mind.

'I'm going to wait and see how she gets on,' Mum was saying. 'I'll see whether she comes out of it a bit, before I say anything about the psychologist. I mean it can't last. It can't be permanent, can it? She can't really believe she's someone else.'

Zan shook his head slightly as he finished his last biscuit. He sat down, elbows on the table, his chin resting on his hands.

'So did the doctor say where it's all coming from, this fantasy? I mean why Janet, for a start, why's she calling herself Janet?'

'She's got a surname now too,' Mum said. 'Bailey. Janet Bailey. But no, we didn't talk about the name. I mean, it doesn't really matter what she's calling herself, does it?'

'It might do,' said Zan, suddenly sitting up straight. 'Think about it. Bailey – next-door's dog! The one Jade's always fussing over, playing with.'

Jade would have loved a pet. They all would but Dad was allergic so they'd never had anything more exciting than a tank of tropical fish and a few stick insects.

'So you think that's where the name's come from,' said Mum, 'a dog? She's calling herself after a dog?'

'Might be,' said Zan, with sudden hope, 'and that's good, 'cos there's like a connection with the real world – even if Jade doesn't get it.'

'We won't need the psychologist, at this rate,' said Mum, attempting a faint smile. 'Just let you sort it out, eh, Zan?'

'Yeah, right!' said Zan. 'I still don't get the Janet bit

though. Who do we know called Janet? Mrs Simmonds in the office at school – she's a Janet. I mean, Jade spent a fair bit of time with her during exams.'

Mum nodded, sharply, as if she didn't want to think about Mrs Simmonds or their school right now. Too many memories of how Jade had struggled in day after day, trying to cope with exams. Coming home totally exhausted but still revising up in her room until turned midnight every night.

'My hairdresser's called Janet,' Mum was saying. 'Jade knows her quite well. And there's Great Aunt Janet, Granddad's eldest sister, the one we used to go and see up in Scotland.'

'Duh!' said Zan. 'I know who she is and where she lived! It's not me that's lost my memory, you know.'

'Jade's not lost her memory,' Mum snapped. 'Not as such. Anyway, I just thought you might have forgotten the details. Aunt Janet's been dead almost seven years now – you'd have been quite young last time you saw her.'

'And Jade would have been about nine, yeah? So were they like close or anything?'

'Not particularly,' said Mum. 'I mean, you all used to like going, with the animals, the smallholding and everything.'

Well, all except Dad who spent the whole time sneezing and guzzling antihistamines!

'And Janet made such a fuss of you all,' Mum said, 'but we didn't go that often and anyway, I'm not sure where this is getting us. It's probably nothing to do with Aunt Janet or my hairdresser or Mrs Simmonds. It's probably just a name Jade's picked out of nowhere. Jade, Janet, they're quite similar, I suppose.'

Zan wasn't sure but there was no point pushing it.

'And have you told Dad,' he asked, 'about any of this?'

'I phoned him, yes. It was a bit hard to explain, on the phone. I think he thought I was exaggerating, at first, but he's going to leave the conference early, not bother with the final session or the dinner,' said Mum glancing at her watch. 'So he should be home in an hour or two.'

'It might help,' said Zan. 'If she's gonna recognise anybody, I reckon it'll be Dad, won't it? Shall I go and see how she is?'

'If you want,' said Mum, 'but don't wake her if she's still asleep.'

Zan headed for the lounge but it was empty. The big, tartan blanket, the one they used to use for picnics, was lying on the floor, next to the settee, but there was no sign of Jade. He hurried back towards the kitchen to get Mum but at the bottom of the stairs, he paused. He could hear someone moving around upstairs. He found Jade on the first floor, standing outside one of the three

19

bedrooms, looking at the sign on the door, the wooden sign that was neatly screwed on.

'Claire's room,' she said. 'Who's Claire?'

'Your sister, my sister, our sister,' said Zan.

'I've got two sisters,' said Jade.

'Yeah, that's right!' said Zan. 'Claire and Gemma.'

Jade shook her head.

'Yeah,' said Zan, desperately trying to prompt her, to encourage any flicker of memory. 'You remember Gemma! Loud mouth. Bossy. And Claire, she put this sign up when she first went to Uni, yeah, like she was saying, "The room's still mine, OK." Like she thought Mum was gonna rent it out or something. Still won't let anyone take it down even though she's got her own flat now. That's why we're both stuck in the attic.'

He paused, hoping that something would get a response, bring back a memory, a real memory. There was a slight change in Jade's expression, as though she was getting something.

''Cos Claire won't let no one have her room,' he went on quickly before he lost her again. 'And this is Gemma's room, look,' he said, moving along the corridor, opening a door.

Jade looked, smiled and nodded slightly.

'Where are they then,' said Jade, 'Susan and Linda?'

'You mean Gemma and Claire?' said Zan.

'Yes,' said Jade, as though she hadn't realised the

mistake, as though the names Susan and Linda had slipped out automatically. 'Where are they? Are they at work?'

Was this for real, Zan wondered. Could she really not remember the people she'd spent her whole life with? Or didn't she want to? Was she burying the good memories along with the bad?

'Well,' he said. 'Claire lives in Leeds, yeah, with Ben. You know, Big Ben – plays rugby.'

'So Claire's married to Ben?'

'No,' said Zan. 'They're not married yet. They keep saying they might but they haven't got round to it.'

Jade looked puzzled, like she'd done about most things today so Zan passed on.

'And Gemma's still at Uni – well, she's in Spain now, working for a bit. But she'll be back before the end of the hols.'

Gemma hadn't wanted to go to Spain at all, after what had happened with Jade, but Mum had said she must. That there was nothing she could do if she stayed at home; that life had to go on as normally as possible. Yeah, right! Let's all be normal, let's pretend it never happened, let's pretend Jade's fine.

'Spain?' Jade said, shaking her head again as she walked into Gemma's room. 'And university? That's not right. Dad wouldn't let them go, he won't let any of us go.'

'You kidding?' said Zan. 'It's all he ever talks about. Why can't you be more like your sisters, Zan? Claire got a first, Zan, Gemma's at Oxford, Zan. Like I didn't bloody know, like I'm ever allowed to bloody forget! Sorry, didn't mean to start a rant.'

But he didn't need to apologise, Jade wasn't listening. She was staring round the room but she wasn't really seeing either. Her eyes were somewhere else, like they'd been earlier that morning when she'd spooked him so much, like they were off on their own, somehow, searching for something, wanting to be anywhere but here and now.

'He says it's a waste of time,' she started saying, slowly, carefully. 'Dad says school's a waste of time. He won't even let us stay on in sixth form.'

Zan didn't know what Dad she was talking about but it sure as hell wasn't theirs!

'So, what else do you remember then?' he asked, sitting on the edge of Gemma's bed.

He wasn't really sure he wanted to know. It was freaky talking to this person who wasn't quite Jade. But if he could get her talking, it might give them some clues, might even start bringing her back. And it couldn't do any harm, could it?

'Nothing,' she said, 'just bits. Things come to me but they don't stay. I remembered my sisters earlier. What they looked like.'

Which sisters though? Was she talking about Claire and Gemma or the made-up ones, Susan and Linda?

'And now I can't,' Jade was saying. 'Now it won't come back. Why are you doing this? Why are you keeping me here?'

'Hey,' said Zan, standing up, arms raised in mock surrender. 'I'm not keeping you anywhere, OK? Come on, let's walk. Show me where you want to go, yeah?'

Zan followed her out into the hall but she didn't go far. She stopped near one of the dozens of bookcases they had scattered round the house and picked up a photo from the top. One of the yucky, embarrassing pictures Mum insisted on having out for everyone to see. The school photo of him and Jade, taken when they were in Years 7 and 9. Jade was smiling but he was scowling, imagining his mates laughing at him for having a photo with his big sister, wondering how many he'd have to thump to knock the smirks off their faces.

Jade looked at the picture. She half-smiled, as though she recognised it, as if she'd remembered him fussing about having it taken but, almost immediately, her eyes took on the faraway look and the smile disappeared.

'This isn't right,' she said, firmly, definitely, as if it was something she was totally sure about. 'There are no boys at my school. I go to an all girls' school, a grammar school, a girls' grammar school.'

'OK,' said Zan, slowly, trying to decide how to play it.

If it was anyone else acting like this, he'd have thought it was a trick, a joke, a hoax. But Jade wasn't really your practical joker type. Jade wouldn't pull a stunt like this even when she was well, even before – no, it had to be real, at least in her own head. Maybe she was picking up on some of Gran's stories here. Gran had gone to a girls' grammar school. She was always going on about it. Dead proud of having been Head Girl, like it was her greatest achievement in life!

'So what was it called then, this school?' he asked, normally, casually, as if this was an ordinary conversation.

'I don't know,' she said, with the same panicky edge to her voice that she'd had earlier that morning, when he'd asked her questions she couldn't answer. 'It's like there's this big whirlpool of fog in my head then sometimes it clears for a minute and I see things – know things. Does that make sense?'

Zan nodded even though it didn't.

'Blue,' she suddenly said. 'The uniform was blue, dark blue, not green.'

She put the photo down, the photo of them in their putrid green jumpers. But the blue made a certain sort of sense. Gran's uniform had been blue. She still had her old navy blue school beret with the stupid blue and white pompom on top, stuffed in a drawer with all her certificates and her precious Head Girl badge!

'Attics,' Jade added, 'we had lessons in the attics sometimes.'

'It was sort of old then, your school?' Zan said.

Older than her real school, anyway, which was flat, box-like and modern. Or was Jade confusing her fantasy school with her bedroom? The attic room where she'd locked herself away, working, revising, blocking everything out.

'Maybe,' said Jade. 'Yes, it might have been old. I'm not sure. There was a massive hall. I remembered that earlier. I saw myself sitting there, doing exams, but I can't really see it now. Like I said, things come and go, some stronger than others. Some things seem to belong here but some don't – like I'm living two lives.'

'So is there anything else?' Zan asked. 'Any other memories that seem strong?'

'You're different,' Jade said, ignoring his question. 'Different to your mum.'

'Well, I hope so, yeah,' said Zan. 'I haven't got a tidiness fetish for a start and I *hate* classical music!'

'You ask questions,' Jade said, 'like you believe me. She just says I'll get better soon, as if I'm mad.'

'She doesn't think you're mad. None of us do, 'cos you're not.'

'You're nice,' Jade said.

25

Zan laughed.

'Nice! That's not what you usually say! You usually say I'm a pain in the butt or worse!'

'You talk funny.'

No, he didn't but Jade did; this Janet version of Jade. He hadn't really noticed it with all the other stuff but now he thought about it – it was hard to pinpoint exactly but she sounded different. She sounded more sort of polite, old-fashioned or formal with a hint of a strange accent. It could be Lancashire or something like that, a cross between Gran and Nana Wallace maybe.

'You've got a lot of books,' she was saying, looking at one of the shelves.

'They're not mine!' said Zan. 'I don't like books. What about you? You like reading?'

She nodded.

Well, at least that was right. At least Janet and Jade had something in common. Or maybe that was just girls. All girls were into books, weren't they? At least the ones he knew: his sisters and most of the girls in his class. He left Jade looking at the books and walked over to the window as he heard a car on the gravel. Dad was back already. He probably hadn't bothered with any of the sessions. He'd probably left the conference as soon as he got Mum's call.

Zan watched him haul his briefcase and his small suitcase out of the boot. Dad didn't bother putting the

26

car in the garage, he just hurried towards the back door, not looking up, not knowing anyone was watching. He had that look on his face, that look he'd had for two months now, since what had happened to Jade. Forehead creased, eyes narrowed, mouth tight, making him look about a hundred years old.

Mum looked older too now but she hid it better. She still highlighted her hair to cover her greying bits, did her make-up, fixed on a reassuring sort of a smile, at least when Jade was in the room. Dad tried, he tried to sound upbeat, tried to hide the anger in front of Jade but it never quite worked. Dad would be up soon. Maybe he'd talk to Mum for a minute or two but he'd want to come looking, to see for himself. Here he was already, footsteps heading towards the lounge.

'We're up here,' Zan shouted.

'Who is it?' Jade asked, dropping the book she'd been looking at.

'It's OK,' Zan said. 'It's only Dad.'

Jade edged back as Dad appeared at the top of the stairs. She stared, like she wanted to know him, wanted to recognise him but it was like there was something holding her back, dragging her back almost. Zan could see the blankness descending. Even worse, Dad could see it too.

3

Janet prowled round the attic bedroom, opening cupboards, checking out drawers, trying to find out about this Jade person, the girl she was supposed to be. She'd come up straight after dinner, pleading tiredness. She'd managed to eat some of the dinner although it had tasted funny at first. Chicken Korma they'd said it was.

'Home-made,' Zan's mum had added, as though it was something really special.

They didn't seem to eat normal food, this family, though Janet wasn't quite sure what normal was. She couldn't remember what she liked, what she usually ate. They'd talked a lot over dinner. Zan's dad had talked about the conference he'd been to, Zan had talked about school. They'd sort of left her alone, hadn't asked her any questions, but they'd kept looking at her, like this was some sort of test, like she was an animal in an experiment or something. Maybe she was. Maybe they were watching her, even now, through a spyhole or the mirror or something. A two-way mirror?

She didn't want to check, to go too near the mirror. Looking in mirrors was scary, almost the scariest thing of all. Instead she sat on the floor and opened one of the low cupboards underneath a sort of desk thing. The cupboard was full of exercise books, school books, folders. She pulled a few out. They had neat writing on the front. Jade Wallace, 11S, Set 1, Maths. Jade Wallace, Business Studies.

Flicking through the work was like everything else; some things she remembered fairly clearly while others were a total mystery. And all the time she was fighting against the fog, trying to push it away, trying to find the images, the memories that were lurking behind it, trying to work out what was real.

One folder she found, a clear plastic one, was full of cards. She pulled a few out. Some said 'Get well' on the front but most just had pictures; flowers or cute animals mainly. She opened one which said *'Thinking of you xxx Millie'* in huge writing, purple ink. Another was from *'Mrs Simmonds & everyone in the office'*. The name, she knew that name, but what office, where? She opened a few more. There were some names she didn't know at all, others that felt sort of familiar and some that brought pictures of people to her mind but nothing she could grasp onto for long.

The cards looked quite new, shiny. There was a tiny one with an embroidered multi-coloured butterfly – '*To Jade, missing you, luv Hannah*'. Who were they, these people who were missing Jade, thinking about her? Why had they sent the cards, what had happened? If she was Jade, why couldn't she remember? Apparently she had a Gran and Granddad, a Nana, an Auntie Lynn and an Uncle Alistair. People she should know!

She opened a big card with a teddy on the front. '*Luv ya. Lewis.*' Lewis. The name made her shiver but why? She dropped it, stood up, left the books, the folders, the cards lying on the floor and started exploring the shelves where all the personal stuff was. Cuddly toys, photos of people and places she didn't quite know, although some of them felt sort of 'right', reassuring even. There were bags full of make-up and boxes of jewellery. Earrings, Jade seemed to like earrings. Tiny studs, long dangly earrings, plain earrings and glittery earrings. Dozens of them, all arranged neatly in little white boxes.

My ears aren't pierced! Another certainty, though she didn't know where the thought had come from. She touched her right ear, felt a small stud. It was the same on the left. Why hadn't she noticed that before, who had put them in, when? Could someone have done that while she was sleeping?

Jade seemed to have a lot of stuff. Every shelf, every

surface was crowded, untidy. There was ordinary stuff like hairbrushes but loads of funny things too. Janet picked one of them up off the little cabinet next to the bed, a small, black plastic case. Buttons with pictures on; strange symbols. She pressed the buttons. Nothing happened. She tried to open the case but she couldn't. She could see it was meant to open, she just couldn't work out how but she had a feeling, a funny feeling, that she'd seen something like this before.

The knock on the door almost made her drop it.

'Yes?' she said.

'It's me, Zan. I've brought you a drink,' he said, as he came in, 'and your tablets.'

He put the glass on the cabinet, pulled a piece of tin foil from his pocket, unwrapped it and showed her four tablets.

'Why?' she said. 'What are they for, why do I have to take them?'

'They're the same ones you had this morning, remember?' Zan said. 'They sort of keep you calm.'

'I *am* calm,' she said, though she knew it wasn't true.

'Shows they work then!' said Zan.

'Why so many?' Jade asked, sitting on the bed as Zan separated out the tablets, the two white ones, the small yellow one and a capsule.

'Dunno, really,' said Zan. 'Mum'd probably be able to tell you. Who've you been phoning anyway?' he asked as she put the black, plastic case on the bed, took the tablets and swallowed them, one by one with sips of water in between.

'Phoning?' she said, when she'd taken all the pills. 'No one, who could I phone, who do I know? I don't even know where the telephone is.'

'Er, here,' said Zan, picking up the black case, sliding it open and pressing a button, making the grey screen light up. 'You don't know, do you?' he asked. 'You don't know what this is. OK, OK, don't get all freaky.'

'I'm not!' she said, but she'd felt her shoulders tense, her face contort, even before she heard the noise, a noise that made Zan pull something out of his pocket; another little case.

'Yeah,' he said to it. 'What you want? No, I told you, I'm not going out tonight, can't be bothered. Busy. See ya then.'

As he put it back in his pocket, Janet remembered where she'd seen one before. Zan's mum had one. Yes, that must be it. Or had she owned one herself, once, when she was Jade? If she'd ever been Jade.

'Do you want to do something?' Zan was asking. 'Watch a DVD – a film? Take your mind off things, help you chill?'

'No. No, I'm fine, thanks. I'm just having a look round. Trying to – I don't know. I'm just looking.'

'OK,' said Zan. 'Well, give us a shout if you want

anything. Is your alarm plugged in?'

He checked a lump of white plastic.

'Baby alarm,' he explained. 'Yeah, I know you're not a baby! It's because of the nightmares. It's connected to Mum and Dad's room so if you start shouting out they can come up.'

Nightmares, they talked a lot about nightmares. Maybe that's what it was. This whole thing was a nightmare. She'd wake up soon. Be Janet again. Or Jade. Not both.

Zan went to the lounge, where he knew his parents would be but he didn't go in. He stood outside the door, listening, wanting to know what they made of it all before he put forward his own idea. They were talking about it, as he knew they would be. What else would they be talking about?

'A week or so,' Dad was saying. 'We're supposed to wait a week or so before she can have a scan! It might be a brain tumour, blood clot or anything. How do we know what might have happened when...'

'Keep your voice down, Doug,' Mum said. 'She might hear you. And anyway she was fully checked out at the time, wasn't she?' Mum added, uncertainly. 'I suppose they might have missed something but it's unlikely. The doctor thinks it's probably more – psychological. Disassociation, he called it.'

'Meaning?' said Dad.

'Dr Carr says it's the mind detaching from something it doesn't want to face. It's a way of suppressing bad memories. I checked it out online as well.'

'She's done more than suppress bad memories, from what I can see!' said Dad. 'The whole bloody lot's gone! She barely knows who she is!'

'Well,' Mum said, hesitantly, 'in the worst cases the personality can eventually split completely.'

'Split!' said Dad. 'You're telling me that Jade's developing some sort of split personality and we're expected to sit back and do nothing.'

'No,' said Mum. 'I only said it *can* happen, in the worst cases, usually after persistent abuse or something like that! Jade's not that bad, it'll pass, it'll wear off, I'm sure it will. And besides we are doing something. This Dr Mitchell I told you about might be able to fit Jade in as early as next week.'

'Next week?' said Dad. 'And what are we supposed to do in the meantime?'

'Keep her calm. And keep ourselves calm, Doug.'

'Calm! If they ever find that bastard...'

It was time to go in, time to stop Dad before he went down that route again. If he carried on shouting, Jade might hear. And she wasn't supposed to. She was supposed to remember in her own time, in her own way, or under the supervision of the psychologist, according to the doctor. She had to remember eventually, she had to confront it, but forcing her to remember might cause more damage, Dr Carr had told Mum.

'I think I was right,' Zan announced, walking into the lounge.

'Right about what?' Mum asked.

'Connections,' said Zan, taking care to talk quietly. 'The stuff Jade's doing and saying, it's not all random, not totally. There are definite links to stuff but it's all from way back. It's like sort of history, I reckon, like she's living in the past.'

'What are you on about, Zan?' Dad asked, wearily.

'It's modern things she doesn't get,' said Zan, 'or doesn't want to get. She knows about phones but not mobiles, TVs but not remotes.'

'So?' Dad said.

'Then she started talking about a school but it wasn't our school, right? It sounded more like Gran's old school, a girls' school.'

Dad was shaking his head, his mouth tightening.

'And the name Jade's made up for herself,' Zan tried. 'Me and Mum were talking about Aunt Janet earlier and I was thinking... She used to tell us loads of stories about the old days, didn't she? All sorts of stuff about how they used to ride for miles on their bikes, how people used to leave their doors unlocked – wide open sometimes.'

'Zan,' said Dad, 'I know you're trying to help but I don't see what you're getting at.'

'No,' said Mum, 'listen to him, Doug. I think he might have something. Aunt Janet always put a real rosy spin on the past, didn't she? She never talked about any bad times. It was all picnics and no wasps, according to Janet.'

'And if I remember some of her stories,' said Zan, 'then Jade would too!'

'Remembering them's one thing,' said Dad, 'but living it all? Getting totally wrapped up in it like this!'

'I know,' said Mum, 'but it makes a certain sort of sense. Well, as much sense as anything. Maybe Jade's retreated into a past that she sees as safer somehow. No crime, isn't that what Janet used to say?'

'We had none of these muggers and vandals in my day!' Zan quoted.

Mum had taken it a bit further than Zan had meant, given more shape to his idea but it was possible – possible that Jade was trying to wrap herself up in a world where bad stuff couldn't happen; a glossy version of the past.

'So you're saying that Jade thinks she's a young Aunt Janet?' Dad asked.

'It doesn't all fit,' Zan admitted. 'I mean Aunt Janet's surname wasn't Bailey and she didn't have any sisters called Susan and Linda, did she?'

'No,' said Mum. 'Why?'

'Just something Jade said earlier. She knew she had sisters but thought they were called Susan and Linda. I suppose she's just mixing up a whole load of things. Family stuff mixed with books she's read or films or stuff from history lessons. I mean, she watches loads of history stuff on TV or she used to. So maybe that's what she dreams about, then wakes up thinking it's real.'

'Possibly,' said Dad, sharply. 'You might be right about where it's coming from but it shouldn't have taken hold like this. It's the intensity that's so scary. I mean, how the hell do we get her out of it? And if we do, when she has to face reality again, what then?'

'Bleedin' hell, our Janet, nose in a bloody book again, what about the washing up?'

'Leave her be, Joe. I can do the washing up.'

'No, she can do it, Cath. She does little enough around the house as it is.'

'She's studying!'

'Studying! Time wasting more like.'

'You should be proud of having such clever girls, Joe. Though Lord knows where they get their brains from. Not you or me, is it?'

'Speak for yourself. I done all right, didn't I, without no fancy exams?'

'Yes, you did all right, in your own way. But we're not all the same, Joe.'

'And Susan's happy enough now, with her kiddies, isn't she? Didn't need no sixth form education to wash nappies, did she?'

'I suppose not. And we can't change things for Susan now. But our Janet's different, Joe. Her teachers say...'

'Don't talk to me about teachers! I've no time for bloody interfering teachers. What do they know about the real world?'

'But Daaaad – if I did well in my exams could I stay on?'

'No! How many times do I have to tell you, Janet? I can't afford to keep you on for another two years. It's time you started earning your keep, like we all have to do.'

'But if I did really, really, really well, even better than our Susan?'

'What is it with you, Janet? Why do you go on and on asking the same bloody thing?'

'I'll keep asking until I get the right answer.'

'Aye, you probably will, lass, you probably will. So I'll tell you what I'll do.'

'What? What, Dad, what do you mean? Dad, Mum, don't go. Tell me. Tell me! Don't go. Where are you going? Don't leave me.'

*

Janet thrust her hand into her mouth to stop herself crying out as the scene dissolved, disappeared, leaving her lying in Jade's bed, in Jade's room again. She'd seen it! She'd seen their living room at home, tried to hold onto it; the glass-fronted cabinet in the corner, the plant on the window ledge, the green-patterned curtains. She'd watched Dad leaning on the door frame, grinning at her, not ever taking her ambitions seriously. Mum in the armchair, feet up on a stool, toes poking out from pink, fluffy slippers.

It was a dream, it had to be, but it was more than a dream, somehow. It was too vivid for a dream, yet not exactly real either. Was it a memory then, a memory of another time, another place? Already the colours, the shapes, were fading until all she was left with were the swirling fog and the feelings – the feelings of love and warmth and safety that couldn't be false. Dad with all his moaning and shouting and stupid, old-fashioned ideas, he was still her dad and she had to find him, had to tell him something. There was something important she needed to tell him, but what?

She sat up. The curtains were open and it was light outside but early; she knew it was still early, without looking at the clock. Before she got out of bed she turned off the baby alarm in case they heard her moving about. Bag, she needed a bag. There were dozens in the bottom of the wardrobe; she'd seen them yesterday. She picked a black cloth bag rather than the more noticeable, colourful ones and threw in some clothes. She picked out some more to put on. She chose a long-sleeved shirt to hide the scars; the scars she didn't want to think about. She picked out creamy beige trousers and flat, black shoes. All the clothes were a bit loose but they more or less fitted. They were even sort of nice in a way, though they didn't feel right, look right, somehow.

Money, where would Jade keep her money? In the purse, in the handbag, on the chair. How did she know that? Had she seen it yesterday or some other time when she was Jade not Janet? This room felt a bit more familiar, somehow, today, almost as if it had always been her room. But no, she didn't belong here, didn't want to be here. It was a trick. Those tablets they were giving her were messing her up. She mustn't take any more tablets, she had to get away.

Where? Where to start? Get out of the house first then go down that long road where they'd driven yesterday, towards the doctor's. She could remember all that, so there was nothing wrong with her mind, her brain, was there? Only she couldn't remember the name of the place, this small town that she was supposed to have lived in all her life.

Zan's door was open but there was no sound, no sign that he was awake. Creep past, slowly, quietly, down both flights of stairs to the back door. They seemed to use the back door mostly, not the front. A back door covered in bolts, catches, locks, all clicking incredibly loudly as she touched them. Quiet, must be quiet.

It was scary to be outside, like this, on her own, not knowing where she was going. She was starting to sweat already; she could feel a prickly rash flaring round her neck, and her legs were heavy, aching, like they didn't want to move. But she had to do it. A dog started barking. It sounded like it was coming from the house next door. She must have disturbed it.

It was still barking. It was going to wake someone soon. They might see her, stop her. She had to move. Now. She had to try. Look for something, someone she knew, something to connect to. There had to be something. A secret door, a magic door back to the real world?

She was too old, too smart, to believe in that sort of stuff, wasn't she? But it was the only explanation she could think of. That she'd had an accident and somehow slipped from her own world into this one.

Or was that crazy?

Was *she* crazy?

4

'Mum,' Zan shouted as he bounded downstairs, 'is Jade there?'

'No,' Mum called back. 'I haven't seen her. She won't be up yet.'

'She is,' said Zan, skidding into the kitchen. 'Her room's empty. I knew it was wrong, I just knew!'

'She'll be around,' said Mum, as though she didn't quite believe it. 'She won't have gone out, not on her own. She hasn't been anywhere on her own since...'

'*Jade* hasn't,' said Zan, 'but if she's Janet? If she's still Janet, we don't know what she'd do. Do we?'

'Check the garden. She might be in the garden. I'll check the house.'

They met up at the patio doors, Mum shaking her head.

'She's not in the garden either,' said Zan. 'I've looked in the garage, the shed, everywhere. We need to phone Dad, phone the cops. And don't tell me to go to school 'cos I'm not. Not till we find Jade.'

'All right,' said Mum, 'all right, let me think. Mobile, let's try her mobile first.'

'No point, it's upstairs. I told you, she doesn't know what to do with a mobile!'

'OK. She's maybe not gone far. We can go and look. No! Someone needs to stay here.'

'You stay,' said Zan. 'Get Dad back from work. I'll get my bike out, have a ride round and see if I can find her.'

He wheeled his bike to the gate. Which way? Towards town, out of town, which way would she have gone? She'd have headed towards town probably but should he try the other way first, just as far as the bridge or the new estate maybe? He set off, looking around as he cycled but there wasn't much to look at, very little traffic, a couple of people out walking dogs, but no sign of Jade. She surely hadn't come this way, he was wasting his time. As he neared the bridge he saw a red car coming the other way. A car he recognised, driven by his Year Tutor, Mrs Prior, somebody he'd usually rather avoid but today he waved, signalling it to stop.

'Alexander!' Mrs Prior said, winding her window down.

Mrs Simmonds was with her. They both lived up on the new estate and often came into school together. Both were looking at him, Mrs Simmonds smiling, Mrs Prior scowling.

43

'Aren't you heading the wrong way?' Mrs Prior said, before he could explain. 'School's that way!'

'I won't be in school,' he told her. 'Jade's gone missing. You haven't seen her, have you, on your way?'

'No, no, I haven't,' she said.

'What do you mean, missing?' Mrs Simmonds asked. 'When?'

'Not sure,' he said. 'Not long probably but we're worried because – well, you know.'

Of course she knew. She might not know this latest development but everyone knew what had happened and Mrs Simmonds knew more than most.

'Look, I gotta go,' said Zan, 'but will you check out school? Just in case she's gone there. I don't think so but will you ask around? Phone Mum if you hear anything?'

'Yes, of course,' said Mrs Simmonds, 'and let me know as soon as you find her.'

Mrs Prior said something too but Zan didn't hear. He was back on his bike, swinging it round, cycling so fast it took Mrs Prior a while to catch up and drive past him. It was easier, quicker this way – downhill – so it didn't take long to reach the house again but he didn't stop, he carried on towards town.

Once there he got off, wheeled the bike for a while, stopped a few people on their way to school and asked if they'd seen Jade. Nobody had. It wasn't a particularly big town but it was big enough – big enough to lose someone if you hadn't got a clue where they might have gone or why. She could be in any shop, down any street, in the park, the library, anywhere. He got back on the bike, cycled round. Nothing! Where would she have headed? He found a place to leave the bike. He hadn't got his chain but what the hell. He walked round for a bit, still nothing. She couldn't have gone home. Mum would have phoned if she'd gone back there. Best to keep looking, what else could he do?

Janet stood outside a newsagent's shop. She knew this place but how? Had she been here earlier that morning? She'd been walking round for ages, looking at things, looking at people, not quite knowing what to do, where to go. It all felt so wrong. The sounds were all wrong; too intense, too loud. It even smelled wrong, though she couldn't pinpoint why. She just knew it wasn't where she wanted to be.

A few of the people seemed to know her, but they'd been sort of surprised to see her. Some had turned away, as if they didn't know what to do, what to say. Others had smiled but their smiles were strange, somehow; questioning, pitying, as if they knew something she didn't. She'd smiled back but hurried on in case they tried to speak to her.

She'd looked for buses but there hadn't been many

and she'd lacked the courage to get on. How could she, when she didn't know where they were going or where she was trying to get to? She'd walked round car parks and down alleyways. She'd even found herself touching walls, pressing, hoping they'd dissolve, give way, and she'd find herself in her own world, the one she remembered from the dreams. But even as she'd pressed, there'd been a voice screaming in her head that this was madness, the sort of thing that only happened in books and stories – secret doors, parallel worlds.

Hungry, she was hungry now. She could buy a bar of chocolate, chocolate would do. She went into the shop, joined the small queue, picking up a bar of chocolate from the stand while she waited. She got Jade's purse out, ready.

'35p,' the man behind the counter said, taking the chocolate from her.

'Oh,' she said, searching through the purse, dropping coins on the counter, while the man picked them up, scowling.

She put the chocolate in her bag, hurrying out, bumping into someone in the doorway.

'Sorry,' she muttered.

'Oh, well, look who it is,' said the woman she'd bumped into. 'Jade Wallace!'

Smallish woman. Plain, round, angry face. Hair unnaturally black. Sloppy clothes. Bulges everywhere.

'Sorry,' Janet said again, sidling out.

'You should be,' said the woman, following her onto the street, 'yer lyin' cow!'

What was she talking about? Not the accidental nudge? Jade, she was talking about Jade. Something Jade had done.

'Don't think you'll get away with it, 'cos yer won't, yer lying little tart,' the woman screamed after her, as Janet moved away, her face burning, the rash on her neck prickling, itching.

People stopping, watching, staring as the woman yelled after her. The words seeming to get louder, more abusive, even though she was running now, running away from the woman.

'D'yer know what we've had ter put up with, 'cos of yer fekkin' lies? Ave yer seen what they've done to mi'fekkin' house? Don't suppose yer care, do yer?'

Was the woman following? Is that why the words seemed louder? She didn't want to turn round, didn't want to look.

'Leave her alone!'

Another voice, a voice she knew but she didn't stop. She hurried on leaving the shouting, the swearing, the arguing but she didn't get far. There were light, quick footsteps behind her. Not the woman, the fat woman couldn't move that fast. Janet stopped, turned, let Zan catch up.

'Jade!' he said. 'You OK?'

The way he said the name tore through her like some sort of electric shock. There was a connection, like she knew Zan, *really* knew him, had always known him. Then it was gone, leaving her with an image of the dark-haired woman.

'Who was she?' Janet asked. 'Who was that woman? Why was she shouting at me? What was she talking about? She called me Jade, like you do. Why?'

'Let's go in here,' Zan said, pointing to a small café she hadn't noticed before. 'We can have a drink. I'll phone Mum. Get her to pick us up. I've left my bike but I can get it later or ask someone to get it for me.'

The word 'bike' made her shudder although she didn't know why. There were quite a few words like that, words or names that seemed to reach out to her through the constant foggy fuzziness in her head, grabbing her, scaring her, confusing her. She watched, waited while Zan got the drinks, made his phone calls, away from her so she couldn't hear what he was saying. Then, when he came back, she asked all her questions again, spilling them out quickly, one after another.

'You really don't know,' Zan said, 'you really don't know what she was talking about?'

'No. Why should I, who is she?'

'No one,' said Zan, a bit too quickly. 'Mrs Mellor, local nutter, drinks too much, don't worry about it.'

'She said I was a liar, a cheap tart. And the way she looked at me – like she really, really hated me.'

'Yeah, well she would,' said Zan. 'She's like that. Always hassling people, she doesn't know what she's saying, half the time. It's nothing.'

'And what did she mean about her house?'

'They had a bit of bother,' Zan said. 'Smashed windows and stuff – vandals.'

All the time he was speaking, she could see he was watching her, looking for a reaction. He was lying, or at least not telling the whole truth, but what was he hiding? What could Jade, this girl she was supposed to be, have done to have made the woman so angry? How could Jade be responsible for vandals smashing Mrs Mellor's windows? Why wouldn't Zan tell her? How did it all fit together?

Janet looked beyond Zan, out of the café window, onto the street. She didn't know which was more confusing, this world she'd found herself in or the one she'd left. Or was it possible that they were both the same? Or that neither existed? Sometimes, like now, she didn't feel like Janet *or* Jade; she just felt empty.

'What are you doing?' Dad asked.

'Nothing much,' said Zan, hastily closing his document. 'Just playing a game.'

It was totally irritating having to use his computer in

the small sitting room that both Mum and Dad used as an office, but they wouldn't let him have a laptop or PC in his room. They didn't trust him, thought he'd be mucking about on the net all the time, gambling or downloading porn or something!

'Looked like a Word document,' said Dad. 'For one amazing minute I thought you might actually be doing some work.'

'Yeah,' said Zan, 'I was, sort of, in-between playing the game. Multi-tasking! It's some preparation stuff we've been given for next year. Thought I may as well do it, take my mind off stuff. Is she any better?'

'Not really, she's worse if anything. I had a bit of a job getting her to take her tablets again,' said Dad, sitting on the edge of the desk. 'I had to stand there, watching, making sure she swallowed them properly, like a bloody prison warder!'

He paused, shook his head, as if he couldn't believe any of it was happening.

'But I don't think,' he said, slowly, 'that she'll try and run off again, not after what happened in town. I can't believe she didn't recognise Mrs Mellor, though. You'd think if anything was going to bring it back, it would have been her ranting and swearing like that. I mean, of all the bloody nerve, as if *they* were the bloody victims!'

The Mellors had become victims in a way; with people taking direct action, smashing up the Mellors' house when the cops didn't seem to be getting anywhere. But Zan didn't want to get into all that, not now, not with Dad. There was no point getting him more wound up.

'Yeah,' Zan said, keen to get the focus back on Jade, 'but it didn't. In fact, it seemed to knock Jade even further back, like she was desperate to block it all out, like she was wishing herself somewhere else. While we were waiting for Mum, she stared out of the window for a bit and then started rambling on about another place, another street and a pub where her dad used to drink.'

'She didn't say where?'

'No, it could have been almost anywhere. Then, by the time we got in the car she was talking more sort of normal. Have you noticed that? The way her voice, her tone and stuff switch from Jade to Janet sometimes within seconds?'

'Sort of,' said Dad, vacantly.

Sort of! How could Dad not notice? It wasn't just the voice or the stuff she talked about that changed; Jade even looked different, when she was being Janet! Her eyes, her facial expressions, the way she moved all changed slightly when Janet was in charge. As Jade she was nervy, anxious; as Janet more edgy and paranoid.

'Nothing's consistent, is it?' Dad was saying. 'She's gone all quiet, withdrawn again now.'

He paused again, looking around for a moment as if he was lost like Jade, in some other world.

'Anyway,' he said, with a sudden briskness, 'there are two bits of good news. The police are going to get some sort of restraining order put on the Mellors, to stop any of them coming up here or hassling Jade in any way.'

'Yeah, well, I hope it works,' said Zan.

He wasn't convinced. What he'd told Jade was half true. Mrs Mellor was a heavy drinker, the whole family were. They were well known for causing trouble; breach of the peace, ABH, driving offences, drugs offences. You could find one of them most weeks on the crime page of the local paper – Mrs Mellor, her partner, the eldest lad, even the younger ones, including Davy who was only in Year 7 but had already managed to get himself excluded twice. They'd never needed much excuse to kick off and now with Mrs Mellor blaming Jade for the attacks, there was no guessing what they might do.

'And,' Dad was saying, 'the second is that we've managed to get Jade an emergency appointment with Dr Mitchell at seven o'clock tonight.'

'Is Jade OK about that?'

'Doesn't seem to care one way or the other,' said Dad. 'I'm not sure she even took in what we were saying. She's completely closed down, off in her other world, I guess. That's what's so scary, that's why Dr Mitchell's made space for her. Anyway we'll have to leave soon. Will you be all right, if Mum and I both go?'

''Course, yeah,' Zan said, trying not to sound too eager.

It was exactly what he wanted. A bit of time to himself, to get on with what he was doing: making a list of everything Jade had said about being Janet. Zan wasn't sure why he was doing it, or why he didn't want his parents to know just yet. It just seemed important to write it all down, try to piece it together. The dreams Jade had told him about earlier, when Mum had asked him to sit with her for a bit, all the names Jade had mentioned, like Susan – the alleged sister. Susan had come up again. Then five minutes later she'd been talking about Claire. As if Claire and Susan were the same person like Janet/Jade!

He waited until they'd left before going back to his document. It didn't look much and there weren't many definite links. He couldn't identify the house or even the street Jade had talked about when they were in the café but he could start eliminating. The house wasn't Aunt Janet's, that was for sure. She'd maybe chosen the name from Aunt Janet but as for the rest – where was that coming from? Did it matter, was it important, how come it seemed so real to Jade?

He could understand why Jade was traumatised, why she'd have nightmares but this new stuff was well weird, way beyond her reaction at the time even. Maybe he could phone Claire, ask if any of it meant anything to her. A place they'd been on holiday, perhaps, when he and Jade had been small, too small to remember consciously? OK so Jade's description hadn't sounded much like a tourist spot but it might be worth checking.

She'd talked about terraced houses, a pub on the corner, a bridge that might have been a railway bridge. Was it a memory from a film or TV programme, *Coronation Street* possibly? Who could tell? He took out his phone and put it on the desk. The problem was, he didn't know how much his parents had told Claire about this latest glitch. Not much, as far as he could gather. He didn't want her panicking, rushing home from Leeds, or did he? It would be good to see her.

Weird that, how everything had changed. He'd never really bothered much with any of his sisters, not even Jade. They were just there, like an irritating background noise, people to get pissed off with, people to wind up. And when they weren't there, when they were out or away at Uni, he'd never thought about them much, never worried about them. But now? Now he worried all the bloody time, knowing how life could change, in an instant.

He was already starting to worry about Mum and Dad and Jade being out in the car, in case they had an accident. He could sort of understand where his parents had been coming from all those years, with their endless fretting:

'*Where are you going, Claire?*'

'*Who are you going with, Gemma?*'

'*What time will you be back, Jade?*'

'*Make sure you've got your phone, Zan.*'

Trouble was you couldn't stop things happening, could you? However much you worried, however careful you were, you couldn't account for random bloody chance, for being in the wrong place at the wrong time. Zan could feel the sickness in his stomach rising up to meet the knot that was tightening in his throat. His hands were starting to shake. Panic attack. Again.

He'd had dozens in the past couple of months. Mainly at night when he'd lie awake for hours just trying to breathe. Or he'd get up sometimes and open the window, hanging his head out, taking in deep gulps of air. Was he going mad, was the whole bloody family going mad because of what had happened? What was he supposed to do, what had the doctor told him to do when it came on?

Diversion, talk to someone, watch something, a comedy, something funny. He got up, went to the lounge, grabbed a DVD, shoved it in, lay on the settee and made himself watch, gradually relaxing, untensing, until the doorbell rang. He glanced at his watch. It was only eight o'clock. It couldn't be Mum and Dad back already. They'd use their key, anyway. Who then? His mates wouldn't call round, would they? They'd phone or text, wouldn't they?

It was still ringing, the doorbell was still ringing. Should he ignore it? No, it could be the cops, coming round to take a statement about this morning, about Mrs Mellor. They'd said they might. He got up. Stopped. Or might it be the Mellors, out to cause more bother? Zan went to the door but didn't open it.

'Yeah?' he shouted. 'Who is it?'

'It's us. We brought your bike back. You asked us to pick it up, remember?'

'Oh, right, yeah,' said Zan, opening the door a fraction at first, just to check, just to make sure, only opening it fully when he saw the bike, with a twin on either side.

The twins must think he was a right idiot, creeping around like that, or maybe not. The twins knew all the details. Jade had been going out with their brother, Lewis, at the time. She'd been round at their house, the night it happened. It was the night of Lewis's birthday barbecue, a bit of a break from revision. It was supposed to be relaxing, it was supposed to be fun, it wasn't supposed to end the way it did!

Jade wouldn't see Lewis now, wouldn't see any of her friends. Sure she'd gone into school to do her exams but someone had always driven her right up to the door and collected her at the end. She'd been given permission to do her exams in a classroom, on her own, with just an invigilator and between exams she'd sat in the little office next to the reception desk, with Mrs Simmonds guarding her, chatting to her, looking after her.

Zan silently took the bike off the twins, nodding at them, dismissing them before wheeling the bike down to the shed. It was funny that, about the exams. Jade had said exams brought back memories of the school hall but she hadn't done them in the hall, had she? And even if she had, their school hall was nothing like the one she'd described. Was that important? Probably not but he'd write it on his list anyway.

Carry on with the list and maybe look up some info about post-traumatic stress and that disassociation thing Mum had mentioned, until his parents and Jade came back. They couldn't be long now. And when they came back, what would Jade be like? Would she have remembered, would the visit to the psychologist have brought the memories back, did therapy work that fast?

Unlikely – but if the memories hadn't come back, didn't ever come back, what would that mean for Jade, for the trial? That's if there ever was a trial, if the cops ever managed to find him. Why was it taking them so long? How hard could it be? Britain wasn't a big country. It was positively crawling with CCTV. They had his name, his description, so why the hell hadn't they found him yet? Had he already left the country or was he hiding out somewhere local, somewhere close? That couldn't have helped Jade, could it, knowing he was still on the loose. Maybe that's what flipped her over the edge; imagining him watching, waiting to strike again. No bloody wonder she was blotting it all out!

Zan felt suddenly cold as he sat down at the computer flicking between his document and the sites about post-traumatic stress.

'*A normal reaction to an abnormal situation*', was one definition.

'*A situation or incident that undermines the victim's trust in normalcy; that breaks down a belief in ordered existence.*'

Yeah, well Jade's experience was all that – and more!

Thousands of people were suffering from it at any one time, one of the sites claimed; thousands going through what Jade was going through or something similar. But was it? Some of Jade's symptoms fitted but not all, not quite. Lots of the sites mentioned dissociation, the blocking of painful memories, but only a couple mentioned something as intense as an alter ego, a Janet.

So was there something else going on with Jade, something even worse than PTS, some other factor? He followed a couple of links, checking out split or multiple personality but he couldn't stay with it. It was too freaky, too scary, far too close to what he was seeing in Jade.

5

'Mum, Dad,' I shout, bursting into the room.

I'm about to tell them – tell them my news – when I realise they're not looking at me. They're not ignoring me, it's worse than that. They really can't hear me, see me.

'Cath,' Dad's saying to Mum. 'You have to eat something, love. You can't go on like this.'

Mum's sitting by the fire, blotchy legs stretched out, slightly open, as if she doesn't care, as if she's lost all sense of dignity. Her head lolls, chin touching her chest. Dad's standing beside her but she won't look at him. And I'm right there in the room with them. But I can't be, can I, because they can't see me. I can't see myself but I know I'm there.

So this is only a dream, isn't it? Like all the others. And I'll wake up somewhere else, as someone else. I'll be Jade again. That's how it seems to work. Dream. Reality. Simple. Only the dreams are too vivid, reality *too hazy. The borders have got mixed up somehow in the fog.*

Susan, whom I hadn't noticed before, walks over and touches Dad's arm.

'It's all right, Dad, I'll sort Mum out. Maybe make her a drop of soup, eh?'

They edge back a bit away from Mum, as though they're actors in a play and I feel for a moment, as if I'm directing, I'm in control. But I'm not – I'm not in control of anything! I've got no part in this, this isn't like the other dreams, the timing's wrong. It's out of sequence. I'm not supposed to be here.

'Thanks, our Susan, I don't know what I'd have done without you,' Dad says. 'She blames me, you know,' he adds, nodding towards Mum.

'No,' Susan says, quietly, as though she's soothing one of her kids. 'No, she doesn't. How could she? It wasn't your fault. It wasn't anybody's fault.'

'What wasn't?' I say. 'What's happened?'

They don't hear me, they don't answer but I know. And the knowledge swallows up the room, my sister, my parents, leaving me alone in total darkness, with the pain, their pain, surrounding me so I can sense it, touch it, smell it, hear it screaming, screaming, screaming.

'Jade, stop it! It's OK, it's all right.'

Zan's voice was beginning to filter through, quiet

and soothing. He was crouched beside her on a blanket, on the grass. She was in a garden, Jade's garden, with Zan. The weather warm, like it had been for ages now. How long had it been since school broke up and Zan had been looking after her? Three weeks, more?

'You dozed off,' Zan said. 'You'd only been asleep about two minutes when you started yelling.'

Two minutes? It seemed longer. It felt as though she'd been away for a long time, like it always did when she had those dreams of the other home, the other place. As though time wasn't constant; like you could pull it, stretch it, distort it. As though she was living two different lives in two different dimensions that kept colliding.

'Yeah, I was dreaming, again,' she said, 'but it was weird, complicated. I was Jade, looking down, watching Janet. Except we were both the same person, feeling the same things and neither of us were really there because Mum...'

'This is Janet's mum, yeah?'

She nodded.

'They couldn't see me, see her, see Janet and it was like I was...'

She stopped and looked at Zan.

'Do you believe in spirits?'

'Spirits, you mean like ghosts and stuff? No, I don't, no way, why?'

'Because I'm thinking, I'm starting to think – what if I'm Jade and this Janet's living inside me? Or what if I'm Janet but Jade's taken over?'

She paused, knowing how crazy it sounded.

'You mean like you're possessed or something,' said Zan, 'like Janet's a ghost?'

Jade nodded.

'No,' said Zan.

'That's what it feels like sometimes. Like there's two people fighting for control, pulling me from one place, one time, to another. And I don't know who's supposed to win.'

'Yeah, well it's definitely not spirits,' Zan said. 'That sort of stuff's just rubbish, innit? It's what they used to say in the old days when they couldn't explain madness no other way. Shit! No! I didn't mean that. I'm not saying *you're* mad or nothing.'

'I know! It's all right. But there've been cases, haven't there, where people have been possessed. Priests do exorcisms to get rid of them. Maybe...'

'No way,' said Zan. 'Don't even think about it. You're not possessed and you don't need a priest!'

She pulled a couple of blades of grass, rolling them into a ball between her finger and thumb. So if it wasn't possession or madness, then what? It wasn't physical, according to the doctors. All the tests had come back negative; no clots, no tumours, no other nasties. She should have been pleased. She *had* been pleased.

And she'd been sort of all right, for a while, hadn't she? More Jade than Janet, on the surface at least. She was still living with the other family in her dreams, almost every night and sometimes when she dozed off during the day as well. But though her head was still foggy, she'd started to feel more kind of connected with this family when she was awake; this mum, this dad and Zan.

Zan had been great, talking to her about family stuff, sitting for ages with family photos, family films, helping her claw back memories which had begun to seem half real. Memories of a Jade who'd been to a zoo, screamed on rides at a theme park, celebrated family birthdays at noisy parties, posed for silly pictures with groups of friends. A popular, normal Jade, a Jade who had a whole history, a past, a life. A really good life if it was all true. But if Jade's life was so flaming good, why did it feel so wrong most of the time?

Zan was always so keyed-up, so pleased when she joined in, focused, remembered, or pretended to. Dr Mitchell had been pleased too. She'd said they were making progress, 'getting there', whatever that was supposed to mean. Remembering something special, that was it! Jade was supposed to remember something important, something she was still blocking out, something that was lost in the fog. She was supposed to access it, confront it, talk it through, Dr Mitchell said.

Janet needed to remember something too but Dr Mitchell said that wasn't so important. Dr Mitchell didn't like talking to Janet. Janet wasn't real, Janet got in the way. They were working on Jade, Dr Mitchell said.

Only Jade wasn't co-operating properly, was she? Jade didn't really like Dr Mitchell, didn't trust her. Jade pretended to feel ill sometimes so she didn't have to go or didn't have to talk when she got there. Jade was holding back. Sure she was remembering more ordinary things but not the important thing. Maybe she couldn't, maybe there wasn't anything to remember. Maybe it was all lies, part of the trick.

Oh God, she was losing it again, she could feel herself losing Jade. She was slipping back to another garden, another place. She didn't want to. Janet wasn't real. They'd all told her that. She had to try. She had to try to keep being Jade.

'Zan,' she said.

'Yeah.'

'I want you to tell me.'

'Sorry? What?'

'I want you to tell me what happened, what I'm supposed to remember.'

'I can't!' he said, his voice almost a squeak. 'I could phone Mum.'

64

'No, it has to be you. I think I'd believe you. I'm not sure I'd believe anyone else.'

He shook his head, making something in her own head start to buzz, crackle, flare like a massive firework going off, flashes of colour bursting through the fog, her two lives merging, colliding again.

'I was right,' she said, jumping up. 'There isn't anything, is there? It's a trick to keep me here. It's all part of the lie and you're in on it, Zan. You're just like them!'

Janet – that was Janet talking! Janet was forcing herself back, pushing Jade away.

'No, listen,' he said. 'I'll tell you, OK. Just sit down. Give me a minute while I pop to the loo, I'm desperate.'

She sat down again, looking at Zan, wanting to believe him, wanting to hold onto Jade, wanting to give him a chance.

'Don't move, OK?' he said, backing away from her.

As soon as she saw him go inside, she stood up again. He was up to something, she was sure. She couldn't trust him. She couldn't trust any of them. No, that was Janet talking again. Fight it, fight, stay with Jade, make him tell her; make him tell her the truth.

Zan darted into the downstairs bathroom, locked the door and took out his phone. He didn't want to risk speaking in case Jade had followed so he sent Mum a text. Jade wouldn't think about that. She'd more or less got the hang of mobiles and computers again, though she wasn't much interested and she still didn't think in terms of texts or emails.

He paused deciding whether to send it. Was he doing the right thing? He was supposed to contact his parents if there were any developments, any changes, but it felt sneaky somehow, like he was letting Jade down. On the other hand he couldn't do what she was asking. He couldn't tell her. He wouldn't know how.

Maybe, by the time he'd finished in the loo, she'd have forgotten she'd asked. It was freaky, one of the many freaky things about the new Jade. Her short term ordinary memory was fine but anything further back or anything about the Janet/Jade business, and her mind was still all over the place flipping in and out of the different lives.

She seemed to have forgotten all about her walkabout in town and Mrs Mellor an hour or so after it happened, like Jade was deliberately blocking it out. Sometimes she'd forget she'd seen Dr Mitchell the minute she got back yet other times she'd remember every word. Not that any of it was helpful. He'd seen the transcripts of some of the sessions:

'I don't really want to talk to Janet today, Jade. Can you make her go away?'
'No.'

'So how do you feel when Janet's around?'

'Confused.'

'Anything else?'

'Safe.'

'And do you feel safe when Jade's on her own?'

'No.'

'Do you know why?'

'No.'

There was no sense to it, no pattern! Jade could go for hours, maybe days, seeming more or less normal; anxious, hyped-up, but definitely Jade. Then Janet would pop up again, usually after a dream, though not always, and the confusion, the paranoia would kick in. She'd start talking about lies, tricks. Like now, or like what had happened on Sunday. Jade had been having a good day on Sunday, brilliant in fact. She'd been talking, laughing even, more like the real Jade, the old Jade. Then in the evening a couple of her mates had called round and Jade said yes, she'd see them. For the first time since it happened, she agreed to see someone other than doctors, police and family.

Mum had brought them through to the lounge – Jade's best mates, Millie and Hannah, whom she'd known since Juniors. They'd edged in, sort of nervous, uncertain, not knowing how to act, what to say. Maybe that's what had set Jade off, maybe she'd picked up on it or maybe they'd just reminded her of the party, Lewis's barbecue. Whatever it was Zan had seen the signs even before she spoke, he'd seen the slight shift in Jade's features, the searching-for-something look in her eyes: Janet's eyes.

'You're not Lydia,' Jade had said, staring at Millie.

'Lydia?' Hannah had said. 'Who's Lydia?'

Jade ignored her, swung round to Mum.

'You said my friends were here,' she'd accused.

'They are,' Mum had begun, knowing, as Zan had, that it was hopeless.

Millie and Hannah had stood there, totally confused while Jade ranted on about Lydia and Barbara, her real friends, from her real school. She'd even named the school this time and Zan had written it down later in his notes. It wasn't Gran's old school as he'd expected, it was one he'd never heard of before. There was something else about that school too, something he'd found out yesterday, but it was too bizarre, too confusing, to think about just now. He needed more time to mull it over.

It hadn't been Millie and Hannah's fault but the more puzzled they'd looked, the more worked up Jade had got, until Mum had more or less pushed the girls out.

'She'll be all right,' Mum had said, as they left, 'but it's best if you don't tell anyone – you know – about what she's been saying.'

68

The girls had nodded but Zan wasn't sure they'd keep it to themselves. They wouldn't deliberately cause more trouble for Jade but they were bound to tell someone. People could never keep their mouths shut, could they? It was bound to get round. How Jade had cracked up. Not that surprising, after what had happened, but if Jade's sanity was questioned? Could things be twisted? Might the Mellors make out that Jade was unbalanced before it happened? Freaked out by exams maybe? That she'd got it wrong, made half of it up, like they'd always claimed? Yeah, as if!

Dad didn't think Jade had cracked at all. He was still convinced it was physical. He couldn't bring himself to believe the test results. He kept harassing the consultant. As if Dad wanted it to be a physical problem because at least with physical you'd know exactly what you were dealing with; there was more chance it could be put right.

Zan shook his head. Why was he wasting time? Physical, mental, it didn't really matter right now. What mattered was getting help. He sent the text telling Mum not to bother replying, just to come home.

'*You did the right thing, Zan,*' he could almost hear Mum saying.

She was always saying nice stuff to him these days. Even Dad went on and on about how great he'd been for looking after Jade while they went to work. His mates thought he was weird, he knew that. The way he didn't go out much anymore, the way he hung around at home watching out for Jade. Well let them, he didn't care. They didn't get it, how could they?

Zan put his phone away and flushed the loo, even though he hadn't used it, just in case Jade was around. He opened the door. As he'd suspected, Jade was there in the hallway, waiting for him. She turned and Zan followed her to the kitchen. She was bright-eyed, keyed up but definitely Jade.

'So,' she said. 'You ready to tell me?'

Zan nodded. She hadn't forgotten. OK, onto Plan B, stall for time. He made a drink, opened the cake tin and slowly cut himself a piece of cake, checking his watch while she wasn't looking. It would only take Mum ten minutes to get home, if she'd got his text, if her phone was switched on. But it would be, wouldn't it? Mum always kept it on now. He took his drink and cake to the kitchen table and sat down opposite Jade.

'It was a Saturday,' Zan said. 'Saturday night, two weeks before the start of exams. There was a barbecue at Lewis's.'

'I know,' said Jade. 'I got this far with Dr Mitchell, remember?'

'But *do* you remember?' Zan said. 'I mean really remember. Or are you just going on stuff people have told you?'

'I don't know. I'm not sure. Sometimes I can sort of see it but it's all fuzzy and I don't want to be there because I feel, I feel...'

'What?'

'Angry, I guess,' said Jade.

She looked at him, as if it was a question, as if she wasn't sure, as though she didn't trust herself.

'Like there was something wrong,' she ventured. 'Like I wasn't enjoying it.'

This was new, wasn't it? Zan was pretty sure she hadn't mentioned feelings before. With Dr Mitchell they'd just talked about who was there, what the weather was like, what they'd had to eat. Or so Mum had said. Shit! Maybe it was starting to come back to Jade when he was here on his own with her. What was he supposed to do if she remembered before Mum got back?

'Is that right?' Jade asked. 'Did I get mad with someone? Lewis? I keep sort of thinking about Lewis. I can picture him sometimes, like he's important, like he's part of something.'

Close. Too close. That's what had started it all. She'd got mad with Lewis. It was nothing or nothing much: just Lewis and some of the lads getting a bit drunk. Mucking around, being loud, stupid and childish. Lewis clowning with his mates, ignoring Jade, or so she'd thought. She'd kicked off at him. They'd started arguing like they'd done a million times before. It shouldn't have mattered. They'd have made up the next day only...

Zan couldn't let Jade go there but he couldn't stop himself. The thoughts, the images rushed into his head. If only she'd stayed where she was, stayed at the party and ignored Lewis mucking about. But she hadn't. She stormed out, set off home. It shouldn't have been a problem. It wasn't that late. It was summer. It was still light. She had her mobile with her. It was only a short walk home.

'Zan,' Jade was saying, 'are you all right? You've gone sort of green.'

'Feel a bit sick,' he said. 'Too much cake.'

'You haven't touched your cake.'

'Too much sun,' he said.

'So something happened at the party?' Jade prompted. 'No! Not the party. It's coming back to me. I think – it's almost...'

She rested her face in her hands, her fingers pressing her temples, as if she was trying to squeeze out the memories. No, Zan silently screamed, as the bile rose, burning his throat. Her head slowly lifted, her hands dropping slightly, pushing together, fingertips touching, like she was saying prayers.

'Riding home,' she said. 'I was cycling home.'

'Cycling?' said Zan, hearing his own voice burst out,

unnaturally loud, turning into a nervous half laugh. 'No. You weren't cycling.'

'Yes! I was,' Jade insisted. 'I saw it, just then, felt it. I was on my bike, on my way home, I know I was and...'

'You don't even have a bike!' Zan said, the relief making him smile.

Wherever she was, whatever she was remembering, it wasn't right. It wasn't that night. He studied her face, her eyes, noting the distant look. This was a memory from somewhere else. This was a Janet fantasy, he was sure.

'So maybe I'd borrowed one – borrowed yours?'

'Jade, you wouldn't be seen dead on a bike, trust me, not mine, not anyone's. You hate bikes, always have. Never got past the three-wheeler stage and you didn't even like that much, Dad reckons.'

A picture pushed itself to the front of Zan's mind. Him aged seven or so, out on the road, doing wheelies, mucking about, falling off, and the bike clattering on top of him, wheels spinning. Jade standing rigid, on the pavement, screaming. He wasn't even hurt, not even a scratch or a bruise. But Jade had totally freaked, had yelled and cried for ages. She'd never liked him playing on his bike, fussed more than Mum about wearing helmets and stuff. And no way would she get on one herself.

'So what then?' Jade snapped. 'If it wasn't anything

to do with bikes, what was it? Tell me! I need to know, Zan. Whatever it is, I need to know.'

No. She didn't. Not all random, not like this. It had to be done properly, carefully. Where was Mum? She should be here by now. She'd promised. If anything happened she'd come straight back, she'd said. No matter who she was with, what she was doing. So where the hell was she? As if in answer, he heard a car horn. She'd have nudged it by mistake as she was getting out. Mum was always doing that. Even Jade-being-part-Janet knew Mum's little signature tune. She stood up, glared at him, as Mum came in.

'You sent for her, didn't you?' Jade said. 'You were never going to tell me, were you? It was lies,' she yelled, tipping over the table, as if it were made of paper not solid pine, as if energy was surging through her in a burst of almost supernatural strength.

The sort of adrenalin-fuelled strength she'd used once before. Tables, chairs, plates, cake tin, glasses, vase, water, flowers, crashed, splintered, spilled onto the floor. All energy gone, Jade sank down, arms wrapped around herself, head tucked in, rocking. Rocking like she'd done that night at the hospital. She'd sat hunched in bed, crying and rocking just like that. And he couldn't stand it. He couldn't stand to see her like that again. He knew he should stay, do something, help Mum, but he couldn't.

He turned and ran out of the house.

6

Zan didn't stop running until he reached the park. He fell onto the grass, his chest burning and his breath harsh. He shouldn't have done it, he shouldn't have left Mum like that to deal with Jade on her own but he couldn't go back, not yet. Instead he waited for his breathing to steady, got his mobile out, phoned Dad, told him what had happened; felt a little less guilty when Dad said he'd get home straight away. Work, which had always been a priority for his parents, had been downgraded, shifted into second place. When Jade needed them, they just walked out. But how long could they go on like that, how long would they have to, when would Jade get better?

He rolled onto his back, lying with his limbs outstretched. Crazy thing was, in some ways, she *had* been better since Janet surfaced. She'd stopped all the manic washing, bathing, showering, that she'd done at the hospital and at home between bouts of revision. She didn't cry so much. She'd stopped sitting for hours, looking at the scars. Maybe she needed Janet. Maybe she'd always need her, like some sort of comfort blanket. Maybe they'd just have to get used to having Janet around.

A sudden loud cheer made him sit up. Over on the far side of the park, on the football pitch, Zan could see a whole load of lads running around, waving their arms. Someone had obviously scored. He got up. He couldn't see them clearly but some of his mates were bound to be there. He could join them, have a kick around, do something normal, just for half an hour.

He started walking slowly towards them. As he got nearer he could see the swarm was made up of four groups. A group of little lads, juniors, were milling round the top goal. Beyond them a few older boys were leaning against the fence, smoking, laughing, swigging cans of beer or Coke. There were a couple of losers from his own year too; Woody and Nicco, hanging out with the 'big boys', trying to look cool.

Zan's mates had set up a game around the near post and in front of them, blocking Zan's route, was the fourth group, the smallest group. There were only three of them but somehow they seemed to fill more space, make more noise, than all the rest. They were kicking cans around, punching each other, yelling and swearing at no one in particular until they saw him.

It was Davy who noticed him first. Little Davy Mellor nudged his brother who wasn't so little – Ricky who was supposed to be in Year 10 except he hardly ever turned up. The third lad was about Ricky's height but broader. Zan had a feeling he'd seen him before, maybe around school, but he didn't know him; didn't want to know him.

Change of plan. Zan turned to go back because no way did he want to tangle with those three. They couldn't do much, not in a crowded park, but Zan didn't want the hassle. He'd only gone a couple of steps when something smacked into the back of his head and, as he swung round, a golf ball dropped at his feet. Ricky was grinning. He was a good shot, hitting his target that hard with something that small, from that distance.

'Hey, Zan,' Ricky said, moving quickly forward, picking up the ball, shoving it in his pocket. 'How's yer sister?'

It was a wind-up, not a genuine question. What did Ricky care about Jade? Zan tried to move round him, to head towards his own mates, who'd stopped their game and were watching but Ricky's friend blocked Zan's path. Davy moved in too, the three of them circling Zan, prowling like hyenas round a corpse. Zan noticed his own mates edging closer, forming a bigger circle. It was OK. Nothing could happen, could it?

There were too many witnesses for the Mellors to start anything daft. Zan tried to breathe deeply, stand still and prepare to bluff it out.

'My mam says yer sister's nuts,' Ricky said, looking for a reaction.

Well, he wasn't going to get one. Zan could feel his fists tightening but he kept his arms down by his side. Just stay calm, wait it out, they'd soon get fed up, drift away. They weren't drifting anywhere yet though. Ricky was staring at him out of cold, almost expressionless brown eyes. His mouth had formed into a sort of cross between a smirk and a snarl.

'My mam says she's loopy,' Ricky said. 'Making things up, for attention, innit?'

Zan swallowed hard. Did they know something? Did they know something definite about the Janet business or Jade's visits to Dr Mitchell? Had Millie and Hannah been blabbing? Had it got back to Ricky? Or was this just the Mellors claiming what they'd claimed all along? That Jade was lying. That yes, Mrs Mellor's brother had been around that night. Sure he might have passed Jade. She might have seen him. But that was all, nothing else. It hadn't happened like Jade said. Yeah right, were they crazy or what? They must have seen the evidence, the police must have told them! How could they keep denying it?

'Just 'cos my uncle's got a bit of previous,' Ricky

said, leaning forward, prodding Zan's chest, 'she thinks she can say all sorts of crap.'

'She didn't know at the time!' Zan said. 'Nobody did!'

He knew he shouldn't be answering, shouldn't be talking about it, but Ricky made out like his uncle's convictions were for parking on yellow lines or something.

'Just 'cos he made some mistakes when he was younger,' Ricky said, 'he gets blamed for everything.'

Mistakes! He'd been sent down for twelve years! He'd come out on parole after six, moved in with the Mellors, then less than a month later... Zan's fingers were still curled over, his nails digging into his palms. Trouble was, no one had known about the previous convictions and what they were for. They didn't know to be on their guard. So when he'd stopped Jade and asked her what time it was, she'd have thought that was all he wanted, just the time.

OK, she'd have been wary, maybe, like you'd be wary of any bloke you didn't really know. She'd maybe have thought he was going to snatch her phone or something. She'd have tried to keep a distance. But she wasn't careful enough. She wasn't concentrating. She didn't know how dangerous he could be!

'But he never did nothing, this time,' Ricky yelled. 'It weren't like she said! Me uncle had nowt ter do with it.'

'So why's he disappeared?' Zan said. 'If he's so bloody innocent, why's he done a bunk? Why won't you tell the cops where he is? So he can explain away all the evidence they've got!'

'We can't tell, 'cos we don't know nothing,' said Ricky. 'He took off when the cops came round. He knew that whatever it was about, they wouldn't believe him, would they? He tries to make a new start but he can't 'cos the cops blame him for everything. They don't believe nothing he says.'

'And why should they?' said Zan. 'She saw him. She recognised him!'

'Bollocks,' said Ricky, prodding Zan again. 'The cops probably put her up to it, showed her his photo or something. Got her to say it was him! They do stuff like that. They tamper with evidence too. There's loads of people put away for stuff they never done. All that forensics and DNA crap – they mess with it, set people up.'

Ricky was prodding, pushing, all the time he was speaking, doing it a bit harder each time.

'You're supposed to keep away from us,' Zan said.

He knew how feeble it sounded, knew he looked a wimp, but he wasn't going to give them what they wanted, he wasn't going to get involved in a fight. The audience was getting bigger now. The little lads had given up their game and crowded round. The older lads, with their hangers-on, had left their fence and were hovering on the edge of the widening circle, expectantly.

Nicco's eyes were opened wide, his face flushed. Woody's mouth was drooping open like a great soppy dog's. Would any of them help him though? Would anybody step in? Or would they just watch, like with playground fights? Zan had done it himself once or twice. Stood back and watched, done nothing.

Ricky was grinning, gearing up, enjoying the buzz. He wouldn't be able to resist. Zan could fight back. He'd have to. But he couldn't win, not against Ricky Mellor. Before he could work out a plan, Zan felt the sudden force of both Ricky's hands thudding into his chest sending him stumbling back. He regained his balanced and instinctively lurched forward, head down, butting Ricky's stomach. It was like headbutting a wall. Colours flashed in front of Zan's eyes, his brain exploded.

'Shit!' he heard someone yell, as Ricky's body melted away and he felt himself slumping face down on the grass.

Car, Zan could hear a car. What was a car doing in the park? It had stopped close by. Voices, Zan could hear loads of lads all talking at once. He felt someone pulling him up. It was the twins and another lad from his year at school. A quiet, geeky type whom he didn't know that well. Chris? That was it, Chris. The rest were all hovering round the police car, round the two cops, yelling thirty different stories, while Zan tried desperately not to puke.

'It's my dad,' Chris said, nodding towards one of the cops. 'I phoned him when Ricky started on at you. Sorry.'

'No,' said Zan, 'it's OK. I mean thanks.'

Geeks like Chris came in handy sometimes!

'He should never have been let out,' Chris said.

Zan guessed he was talking about Ricky's uncle.

'That's what my dad says, anyway,' Chris added. 'Not after what he did to them other two girls.'

Zan nodded. A lot of people were saying that now, when it was too late. But how could you tell? How could you know whether someone had changed, whether they should be let out early? They had procedures the cops had told them about: parole boards, psychiatric reports, prison reports. It was all carefully assessed. Only sometimes they got it wrong.

'Well, they won't let him out next time,' Chris said.

Chris sounded so certain. Did he know something Zan didn't? Something he'd picked up from his dad, maybe? Were the cops closing in, did they know where Ricky's uncle was hiding? As far as Zan knew they were checking out all his old prison mates, keeping watch on the airports and stuff, getting absolutely bloody nowhere. It had even featured on *Crimewatch* but all the alleged leads and sightings had fizzled out.

And even if they picked him up, would the case stick? Could Ricky's uncle really make out he'd been framed, set up, like Ricky reckoned? Could he wriggle out of it despite all the evidence or was that just the Mellors' wishful thinking? Zan's head was still throbbing from its contact with Ricky; beating out a rhythm to the questions that went on and on.

What if the Mellors were right? Ricky had sounded so definite, so certain. What if Jade had been mistaken? Confused, like she was now? What if she'd identified the wrong bloke? No, not possible, there was already too much other evidence and no way could it be a police setup. Why the hell was he even thinking about it, why had he let Ricky get to him like that?

'Are you all right, Zan?'

Chris's dad was speaking. Zan nodded.

'We'll take you home,' Chris's dad said.

'No,' Zan said. 'I'll walk. I'll be OK, honest.'

'Well, get some of your friends to walk with you, just in case,' Chris's dad said. 'Although I don't think they'll be any more trouble today. We'll be talking to Ricky as soon as we track him down and I'll send someone round to take a statement from you, later, OK?'

Zan nodded again. His head was aching big time now. Why had he said he'd walk home? He didn't have the energy to speak properly, let alone walk. Somehow he managed, trying to ignore his mates who were all hyped-up, gibbering, going over what they'd heard, what they'd seen. Even Nicco and Woody had tagged along.

'Did yer see it?' Woody kept saying. 'The way he headbutted Ricky, did yer see it?'

Some of the saner, calmer ones kept asking questions; questions that Zan ignored, pretending he hadn't heard. He'd have no mates left at this rate but he didn't really care. At the bottom of his road, he told them he'd be all right and they drifted off. He needed a few minutes on his own before he got home, a bit of time to wind down.

He'd been walking with his head down and when he looked up, he saw someone on the other side of the road, opposite their house, watching it. A lad with a cap pulled down, shading his face. Was it Ricky? Had Ricky got here before him, watching, waiting for him? Grey top, dark jeans, was that what Ricky had been wearing? Zan couldn't remember, couldn't be sure and definitely didn't want to find out. He turned, started walking back the other way.

'Hey!' the lad shouted.

Zan started to walk faster. He didn't want to run but he couldn't help it. As soon as he heard the footsteps behind him, he set off but not quickly enough. The lad had grabbed him. Zan swung round, kicking out as he felt the grip on his arm.

'Bloody hell, Zan, what yer doing?'

'Me?' said Zan, clutching Lewis as he tried to regain his balance. 'It's you, you great moron! Creeping around, scaring me half to death.'

'I wasn't creeping,' said Lewis, 'I was just passing. Thought maybe I'd try – but I knew she wouldn't see me, so I was sort of still thinking when you turned up. I just wanted to know how she is.'

'Couldn't you phone?' Zan snapped. 'Sorry,' he added. 'It's bin a crap day. And Jade's still not good.'

A bit of an understatement but it was all Zan could manage.

'Yeah,' said Lewis. 'Hannah mentioned the other day that Jade was a bit – I mean, that's why I came. I – look, just tell her I was asking, OK?'

Zan nodded but he knew he probably wouldn't. There was no point. Jade wouldn't respond, just like she hadn't really responded to most of the other calls and messages they'd told her about over the past few weeks. When he got in he was just going to crawl off to bed but, as he headed for the stairs, he heard raised voices coming from the small sitting room. He went and stood in the open doorway but his parents didn't notice him. Dad was at his desk, doing something on his laptop. Mum was standing behind him, looking at the screen, shaking her head.

'It must be here somewhere,' Dad was saying.

'Maybe you misheard,' Mum said. 'You were driving,

so maybe you weren't listening properly.'

'What?' said Zan, stepping into the room. 'What are you looking for?'

Mum moved towards him, gave him a quick hug.

'You OK?' she asked.

'Yeah,' he said.

'You don't look it,' she said. 'You look terrible. Is that a bruise?'

He shrugged and pulled away. He didn't mention Lewis or Ricky or the park. He'd tell them later.

'Where's Jade?' he asked.

'In bed,' said Mum. 'I got the doctor out just before your dad got back. He gave her a sedative.'

'That's half the bloody trouble, though, isn't it?' Dad snapped. 'She's doped up to the bloody eyeballs. No wonder she's confused, no wonder she's hallucinating and if I'm right...'

'Your dad thinks he heard an item on the radio on the way home,' Mum said.

'I don't *think*,' said Dad. 'I know. I'm trying to find it online.'

'Find what?' said Zan.

'A new report,' said Mum, 'about a brand of anti-depressants causing hallucinations and even...'

'Suicides,' Dad snapped, as Mum paused. 'Teenagers mainly – attempting suicide, especially when the drugs are taken in combination with other stuff.'

'And you think these tablets might be the ones Jade's on?' Zan asked.

'I know they are,' said Dad. 'I heard the name. And the bloody doctor increased the dose, recently, didn't he? I mean, is he trying to bloody kill her or what? Got it, look, it's here.'

Zan and Mum turned to look at the screen. Dad was right. The tablets named were the ones Jade was on. And Dad was right about the amount too. The doctor had doubled the dose when the Janet thing kicked in! So was that what it was all about? Were the drugs causing the dreams, the erratic memories and the disorientation? That was one of the words the report used. Disorientation. Was that what was making them seem so real, so powerful?

'It's not an official report,' Mum said, hesitantly. 'It's early days. They're only quoting a few cases. The makers are disputing it.'

'Well, they would, wouldn't they?' Dad said. 'Bloody pharmaceutical companies! All they care about is money. But it's enough for me. Jade's not having any more. I'll get on to the doctor. Get them to prescribe something else, if they must. Bloody hell! Don't they test these drugs, or what?'

'Of course they do,' said Mum but Dad wasn't listening.

He'd already stormed out, heading for the house

phone probably to yell at the doctor. Mum shook her head again then followed him. Zan stared at Dad's laptop for a while longer, scrolling down. Jade was certainly showing about ninety per cent of the side effects the report mentioned, though mercifully not the big one. She hadn't tried to harm herself. There was no hint of anything like that.

But would the drug's side effects really explain everything? It made sense and a couple of days ago Zan might have thought so. Except now there was the business of the school – Janet's school. Although maybe he was mistaken about that, seen what he'd wanted to see.

He left Dad's laptop, walked over to the other desk and switched on his computer. He loaded his own document first, checked the name of the school Jade-being-Janet had mentioned. He googled the name, as he'd done yesterday. Why had he done it, why had he bothered, what was he expecting to find?

The name wasn't that common so only dozens of results popped up, rather than hundreds. A school in Essex that was quite modern and nothing like the one Jade had described. Another in Hertfordshire, which partly fitted what Jade had said but not totally. He ignored those and went straight to the website of the one he'd found yesterday.

It was on the outskirts of Manchester. It was a mixed comprehensive now but it used to be a girls' grammar school. Before that it had been a small, private boarding school. The school seemed quite proud of their history. They had a whole section on it, with photos and everything: girls with plaits, ankle socks and blazers. The style of uniform had changed over the years but the colour hadn't. It was blue, dark blue as Jade had said. And, although much of the school was new, the main building was built in the late 19th century and looked very much like the school Jade had described – Janet's school.

Coincidence, it had to be, didn't it? If you asked a bunch of random people to make up, to imagine a school from the 40s, 50s or 60s, they'd come up with something like this. Ask them to make up a name for the school and you'd be almost sure to find a real one that fitted, somewhere in Britain. Jade's rambling didn't mean anything. Why was he looking again? It was mad, completely mad. On the other hand, there was that stuff Jade had said earlier about being possessed, about feeling like there was a battle for control. So maybe it was worth trying one more thing, following up an idea.

He couldn't do it now. He wouldn't be able to access the site he needed. But Mum could. He could do it if he logged on as her. OK, so first he had to wheedle a few bits of information out of Mum. No point trying just yet, she was busy out in the hall still talking to Dad about Jade's medication. Besides, when he did get their attention, he really needed to tell them about Ricky and the park first before the cops turned up to take a statement. He hovered for a minute or so before giving up. May as well check on Jade, do something useful while he was waiting.

'Ah, Barbara, how did you get on?'

'Didn't quite finish the last question but I think I did all right on the rest, Miss.'

'I'm sure you did, Barbara. And you'll definitely be doing it for A level?'

'If I pass, yes. Sorry, Miss, I'll have to go or I'll miss my bus.'

'That's all right, dear, you run along. Now what about you, Janet?'

'I don't catch the bus, Miss. I've got my bike.'

'I didn't mean that! I meant how did you get on in the exam?'

'Oh. Fine, I think.'

'But I don't suppose I can persuade you to do it at A level?'

'No. I like history, Miss, but I'd want to do sciences, if I could stay on.'

'If? But I thought the Head had spoken to your father, Janet.'

'She did, Miss but I think . . . '

'What, Janet? You may speak freely and in confidence.'

'*I know she didn't mean to but I think she made it worse, Miss. He was really mad when he got home. Still, I don't think he'll break his promise.*'

'*Promise, what promise, Jade? Jade, can you hear me?*'

'*Zan, what are you doing here? You can't be here. This is my life, Janet's life, not yours and Jade's! You can't just barge in like that! Miss! Tell him. Tell him to go.*'

'*But he seems such a nice boy, Janet. Shall we let him stay?*'

'*This is stupid. You're not my teacher! You're not real. This is all a dream again!*'

'*Of course I'm real. Don't upset yourself, Janet. Look, you're burning up. I hope you're not sickening for something, sickening for something, sickening for something . . .*'

Zan looked at Jade, thrashing around in the bed, shouting about promises in her sleep, face burning, dripping in sweat.

'Jade,' he said again. 'Jade, wake up, can you hear me?'

He touched her shoulder. She squirmed, rolled over away from him but she didn't wake up. Zan hurried back to the door.

'Mum! Dad!' he shouted. 'I think you'd better come up.'

Zan lay in bed totally exhausted but he couldn't sleep.

There was too much buzzing round his head. They'd got the doctor out to Jade again. He hadn't seemed too worried about the fever.

'Just something that's going round,' he'd said. 'She'll be fine in a day or two.'

But it was clear he was worried about the other business, the dodgy antidepressants, not least because of the way Dad had been ranting around, threatening to sue. Dad, who hardly ever used to swear or shout, now hardly ever stopped. He couldn't watch the news without kicking off about the medical profession, the government, the police and attitudes to crime. That was another thing! The police had turned up to take a statement before he'd had a chance to tell his parents about Ricky and the park. It had set Dad off again, in a rant about how there wasn't a strong enough police presence on the streets and how they were too busy filling in paperwork to be bothered catching criminals. How the parole service were understaffed, overworked, making mistakes, letting people like *him* out – nobody caring who got hurt.

Mum had eventually managed to get Dad out of the way so the cops could take the statement in peace and it had all been fairly routine, no problems, except that now Zan couldn't get Ricky's leering face out of his mind. The way Ricky had goaded him, taunted him, like it was some sort of game!

Did Ricky really believe what he was saying about his uncle being innocent? Did he really think Jade would make it up, pretend it was Ricky's uncle if it was someone else and that the police would muck about with evidence? Would Ricky rather believe all that crap than face the truth?

Maybe he would. No one would want to believe that a member of their family was a monster, that they could have done what Ricky's uncle had done. But you couldn't keep denying it for ever! It wasn't like this was the first time. It was the third; the third time Ricky's uncle had done something like this. The other two girls were younger than Jade. One of them had been only twelve for heaven's sake. And those were only the ones he'd been caught for. There might be others.

Why? What the hell made blokes do stuff like that? What made families like the Mellors protect them? Keep on protecting them, letting them get worse and worse until...

Zan lay back, closed his eyes. He saw Jade as she'd been that day when those people brought her home. Her clothes ripped, blood everywhere, crying, hysterical, unable to speak, barely able to breathe. Then later the glazed eyes, the rocking, the first whispered words:

'He had a knife.'

7

Jade sat up in bed, taking the tray from Zan.

'You hungry?' he asked.

'Yeah,' she said. 'I think I am. I feel a lot better today.'

She picked up the spoon and took a sip of the soup. It tasted good but she didn't want to rush it. She hadn't eaten for a couple of days, since the temperature and sickness kicked off, so her stomach felt a bit tight, a bit sore.

'And I don't think I've been dreaming,' she said between sips. 'I don't feel so exhausted.'

'You're looking better,' said Zan, 'not so red. Temperature's more or less back to normal, the doctor reckons.'

'So what was it?' she asked. 'Have they said?'

'It was just a bug. There's a lot of it around but it got more of a grip with you because you were rundown to start with.'

'Rundown! Bit of an understatement.'

'Yeah,' said Zan, rummaging in his pockets, pulling out two crumpled sheets of newspaper, 'but you'll be better now they've taken you off some of the tablets. Look at this.'

He smoothed the sheets, spreading them out on the bed for her to look at.

'It's in all the papers now,' said Zan. 'The tabloids have gone mental about it. And the tablets have been withdrawn for further tests. Your tablets,' he stressed, 'the antidepressants.'

Jade peered over her tray, scanning the newspaper articles, though she needn't have bothered as Zan was still rattling on, explaining it all.

'So you're saying the tablets could have caused the dreams?' Jade said.

'Yeah,' said Zan, 'and the partial memory loss, hallucinations, all of it! Well, most of it.'

'So now I've stopped taking them, there'll be no more Janet?' Jade said.

It felt weird somehow, the thought of losing Janet; like she was losing part of herself. Herself! She was thinking of herself as Jade. That was good, wasn't it? But did she really want to be Jade?

'And I'll start to remember?' said Jade, hesitantly. 'All the things Jade's, I mean I'm, supposed to remember?'

'They reckon, yeah,' said Zan, quietly, 'maybe not all at once but soon, yeah.'

'What day is it, Zan?' she asked, as a random thought came to her.

'It's Wednesday, why?'

'And what's the date?'

Zan told her.

'Results,' she said. 'The exam results are due, aren't they? On a Thursday. Tomorrow, is it tomorrow?'

'Yeah,' said Zan. 'Brill! See you're starting to remember more stuff already.'

But Jade could hear something in his voice, something that made him sound uncertain, worried even. Was he worried about the results or about the other thing? The thing she hadn't remembered yet, the thing that might come back if she let Janet go away.

'Do you think I could go?' Jade asked. 'Pick them up myself, if someone went with me? Would Mum and Dad let me?'

It felt right saying the words Mum and Dad – Zan's parents, her parents. For the first time in ages her mind felt clear. Well, fairly clear, like there was only a light mist now instead of the dense, dark fog.

'Don't see why not,' Zan said. 'If you're still feeling OK tomorrow, I'll go with you, eh?'

Zan left Jade with her lunch and the pieces of smoothed-out newspaper. It was scary, completely unbelievable how much damage tablets could do – or maybe not. His granddad had some major hallucinations once, when he was on morphine after an operation. He'd been convinced there were bats flying round the ward. Not just ordinary bats either but huge vampire bats swooping down, trying to attack him. And it wouldn't be the first time, Dad had said, that pharmaceutical companies had messed up, released something onto the market that caused massive side effects. In fact, Dad had found dozens of examples, obsessively tracking them down on the net.

Zan stopped outside the sitting room. No, there was no point checking again, not now that the tablets explained everything. He went in anyway and sat down but he didn't turn on his computer. He stared at the blank screen picturing what he'd been seeing in the last couple of days when he'd followed up his idea; his stupid idea about that school.

He'd managed to wheedle the information out of Mum, with her barely noticing what he was asking, and used her details to log on to Friends Reunited. He'd found Janet's school, or what he thought might be Janet's school. He'd ignored the more recent leavers, started checking people who'd left in the fifties, sixties and seventies, some who'd be drawing their pensions by now!

It was amazing how many people were registered from back then and there were loads called Janet, Lydia, Barbara, Susan and Linda. All the names Jade had mentioned were there but then they were the most popular names from that time, weren't they? The girls, the women, all seemed to be listed with their original names, their maiden names, but there was no Janet Bailey.

Had he expected one? He wasn't sure but he'd found a Susan Bayley, two years apart from a Lydia Bayley. It didn't quite fit with what Jade had said. The sisters were supposed to be called Susan and Linda. Lydia, allegedly, was Janet's friend. But it was close enough to spook him.

He stood up and headed outside. Was madness catching? How the hell could the Susan and Lydia Bayley listed have anything to do with Janet or Jade? They probably weren't even related to each other, let alone the fictional Janet. Anyway, even if they were sisters, what did he think Jade had been doing, tapping into their memories or something like some freaky alien from *Dr Who*? Sucking their brainwaves through the ether?

He'd known it was nuts but he hadn't been able to resist reading their details. Lydia hadn't written anything about herself but Susan, it seemed, had married, had three children, got divorced, re-trained and was now doing something with finance in Liverpool so not exactly any big clues there. You could read entries like that a hundred times over. He'd done something else too, something a bit more than looking at their details. Something so stupid, he could feel his face redden as he thought about it.

Oh, well, it didn't matter. None of it mattered now. Janet seemed to have gone. No tablets, no Janet, case proved, end of story. They could stop worrying about Jade living in the past and concentrate on the future.

By nine the next morning Jade was up, dressed and pacing round the kitchen.

'Why don't you sit down?' Zan said. 'You can't get them till ten.'

She sat down, tapping her fingers on the table. Fingers with the nails bitten down, the skin at their bases ripped where Jade had picked at it. But apart from the nails, she didn't look too bad considering the bug and everything else. Nervous but then everyone got nervous about results. Claire had been almost hysterical by the time her A-level results had come out and Gemma had actually thrown up when she got her GCSEs. Well, ten A*s were a bit vomit-inducing, he supposed.

'I don't even remember doing them,' Jade was saying, 'not really. I can't remember a single question I answered. Zan! What if I didn't, what if I didn't answer anything? What if I was so zonked out on the drugs that I wrote a load of rubbish or nothing at all?'

'You'd fail,' said Zan, smiling, 'but you won't, I

know you won't. It'll be OK, honest. Come on, let's go, we can walk dead slow, go the long way round.'

'OK,' she said, 'I'll just go to the loo and get my bag.'

Zan wandered into the lounge, switched on the TV while he was waiting, zapping through the channels, just for something to do. There was a cartoon, a chat show, nothing that kept his attention. He flicked to a news channel. He was about to zap again, especially as what he was seeing was a crime scene with police tapes around a section of parkland. A body had been found, they were saying, in Nottingham. He tried to press the remote, tried to tune out, but somehow he couldn't. It was a young girl, the reporter said, a young girl with multiple stab wounds.

Another nutter, another victim! No name was given, there was no description, no details but it was enough to make Zan feel sick, for the girl, for her family, for Jade.

'He had a knife,' Jade had whispered over and over. 'He said he was going to kill me. He had a knife. I thought I was going to die.'

He hadn't killed her but the bastard had done enough! No bloody wonder she was so screwed up.

'I'm ready.'

Zan switched off before Jade came in, like they'd switched off every news item, every programme to do with crime since it happened. Nobody watched cop programmes or even hospital dramas now; it didn't seem like entertainment anymore.

'Yeah, OK,' he said, forcing a smile as he turned, 'let's go.'

They were early but then so was almost everyone else. Zan hung back, for a while, by the school gates. He didn't want it to look as though Jade had a minder, as though she couldn't manage on her own. He kept watch though as she made her way up the drive with Hannah and Millie, seemingly chatty, normal. He found himself crossing his fingers, hoping it was Jade who was talking, not Janet. But it would be, wouldn't it? Janet had gone.

Once the girls got near the school, Zan walked a little way up the drive, watching as Mrs Simmonds limped out of the main doors, leaning heavily on her stick. She must be having what she called one of her 'bad leg days' because she didn't use her stick all the time, in fact some days you could barely tell there was anything wrong at all. Today though, she was moving slowly, carefully. She lifted the stick slightly, pointing it, shepherding the crowds into some sort of order. She had more control than half the teachers! Nobody messed with Mrs Simmonds.

She was OK though, was Mrs Simmonds, more than OK. She'd been brilliant with Jade during the exams. She was talking to Jade now, just for a second or two before hobbling back to the doors, allowing the now orderly queue inside.

Within minutes the first batch were coming out, unfolding bits of paper. One girl hurried past him in tears, a lad mumbled that his dad'd kill him, but mainly people were shrieking, jumping, hugging. Zan zipped up his jacket. It was quite chilly, considering it was still August, with grey clouds coming across as if it was about to rain.

He checked his watch as more and more people came out, blocking his view of the entrance. 10:09 but there was still no sign of Jade or her friends. He moved a little closer, stretching, trying to see. He didn't see Jade but he saw someone else. Ricky Mellor! What the hell was he doing here? He was Year 10 not 11. He barely came to school even when he was supposed to, so why was he here now? He was standing with another lad, the lad from the park. Maybe he was in Year 11. Yeah, that was it. The mate was unfolding a result sheet. Hopefully he'd look at it then go before Jade came out.

But Ricky and his mate showed no sign of moving. The mate was shouting, announcing his crap results, as if it was a competition, as if he was daring people to have done worse. He was laughing unnaturally loud, swearing, drawing everyone's attention. There were a couple of teachers who'd just arrived but they didn't do anything, didn't move Ricky and friend on.

Zan edged closer. He didn't want to get too near, not near enough for Ricky to spot him, just near enough to grab Jade when she came out. Too late, Ricky had seen him. He was coming over.

'D'yer wanna know what 'appened last night?' Ricky said. 'Or der yer know already?'

The answer to both questions was no but Zan said nothing, he was too busy watching the door, hoping Jade wouldn't come out while Ricky was around.

'Dog shit through the letter box,' Ricky said. 'An' a note sayin' stuff about me uncle. Mam's a wreck with it all,' Ricky added. 'Council won't replace no more windows, we've changed the phone number a dozen times and we still get nutters phoning up.'

Zan glanced at Ricky, who looked genuinely pained, genuinely bemused, as if he didn't know what all the fuss was about, didn't know why people were so angry. Zan tried to feel some sympathy, tried to understand, to connect with Ricky on some level, but he couldn't, not really. What was happening to Ricky's family was wrong, he could see that. But what had happened to Jade was worse, far worse. It had stirred up some strong feelings in the area, not just amongst friends but with people who didn't even know Jade.

There'd been letters to the local paper, petitions to the government asking for yet another change in the law. Demanding something like that Megan's Law in

America so you'd know if there was a paedophile or sex attacker living close by. Not everyone had gone down the legal route though. Some had gone a bit mad. The uncle wasn't around so they'd hit out at the family, were still hitting out, by the sound of things.

So tough! Zan shook his head, trying to shake the thought away. Violence was never right, his mum said. It only made things worse. The people targeting the Mellors were way out of line, just thugs, Mum added. But on the other hand, the Mellors hadn't exactly fallen over themselves to help, had they? They knew where he was, they had to!

Ricky knew something, Zan was sure. He wanted to grab hold of Ricky's throat, squeeze it, shake it, force the information out but he couldn't. He couldn't start any trouble with Jade about to turn up at any minute, even if he had the guts to stand up to Ricky, which he didn't. It was cowardice that was stopping him; not any sense of right or wrong.

'An' all because of her bleedin' lies,' Ricky was saying.

There it was again, the total denial! Zan looked towards the entrance, hoping to attract the attention of a teacher but the only two that were around were now dealing with Ricky's mate who was swearing, lashing out at them. Great, just bloody great! Jade was coming out of school now with Hannah and Millie and like everyone else, their eyes went first to Ricky's loudmouthed mate. Hannah and Millie quickly moved back and started opening their results.

Jade looked round, saw Zan, started to walk towards him but stopped when she saw Ricky. She stared as if she knew him or half knew him or thought she ought to know him. Zan moved towards her, grabbed her arm, steering her away quickly before Ricky could kick off.

'Come on,' Zan said, as Ricky spat at them. 'Let's go.'

Jade looked down at the huge globule of murky, grey spit that had landed at their feet, then looked at Zan as if he'd just woken her from one of her freaky dreams. She walked down the drive beside him, a bit too quiet, a bit too zombie-like. Was something starting to come back? Ricky looked a bit like his uncle. Much younger, of course, but the whole family had a similar look about them – dark hair, sallow skin, big-boned. Might Ricky have sparked a memory?

'Let's have a look then,' Zan said when they were halfway down the drive, away from everyone. 'Results,' he added, when she stared at him blankly.

He pointed to the piece of paper in her hand. If he could get her to look, take an interest, it might distract her from thinking about Ricky, at least until they got home. She stopped, slowly opened the piece of paper, looked at it, looked at Zan, glanced back up the drive, shook her head, then set off running towards the gate.

'Jade!' he shouted, setting off after her, when there was no response.

He had no idea Jade could run so fast. She was out of the gates already, running straight onto the road! A car stopped. Mercifully it was a 20mph zone so the car had only been crawling. Jade didn't even seem to notice it. She'd stopped running and was looking around, turning in circles in the middle of the road, as if she had no idea where she was. Other cars had stopped behind the first, the drivers looking almost as confused as Jade, as Zan hurried towards her and steered her back to the pavement.

'They're not right,' Jade was saying, ripping the sheet of paper, dropping the pieces on the ground. 'They're not right, it's all wrong.'

Zan bent down, picking up the bits of paper. He glanced at Jade as he tried to fit the pieces back together. Why was she so white, why was her hand shaking? Had she really screwed up, failed them all? Well, so what? The school would understand, make allowances, what did it matter? It was only exams.

He managed to hold the pieces of paper together long enough to see the grades, before shoving them in his pocket. There were two As, one C and a whole load of Bs. OK, so they weren't quite what Jade could expect at best. She'd been predicted mainly A grades or A*s but they were bloody brilliant considering.

The sort of results he'd kill for!

'Jade, they're fine,' he said, as she stared at him, shaking her head.

'This isn't right,' she insisted. 'I know! I know what happened.'

She'd turned even paler, if that was possible. So maybe this wasn't about results. Maybe this was about Ricky, his uncle, what happened that that night.

'I remember,' Jade was saying. 'I got them. I got them all, all nine.'

'You *have* got them,' said Zan, trying to draw her back from wherever she'd retreated to. 'You've passed. More than passed! They're good, Jade.'

'I'm not Jade!' she screamed.

He knew that. Part of him had known from the moment she'd started running down the drive. The tablets were probably still in her system. That and the shock of seeing Ricky, not to mention the stress of results heaped on top of the other stuff, no wonder she'd freaked again.

'They're supposed to be Grade 1s,' Jade said. 'I got nine. Nine Grade 1s. That's what I had to tell him, that's where I was going!'

Old exams, she must be talking about the old exams. O levels, not GCSEs. Were they graded by numbers not letters, the exams the mythical, or not-so-mythical, Janet would have taken?

107

'Tell who?' said Zan, starting to walk slowly away, hoping Jade would follow.

So far her yelps and screams hadn't attracted too much attention from people milling about on the pavement, walking home or getting into their parents' cars. They weren't that much different to other people's yelps as they studied their results but he needed to get her home before it got out of control. His plan worked. She walked beside him, talking but all the time looking around as if she was in the wrong place at the wrong time.

'My dad,' she was saying, 'he promised! He said if I got all top grades, nine Grade 1s, I could stay on. He didn't think I would, he didn't think I could do it but I did. But ...'

'He went back on his promise?' Zan tried.

'No! He wouldn't do that!' Jade snapped, as though Zan should know. 'I wanted to tell him, straight away. I was on my bike but I didn't go home, I went, I went ... where did I go? What happened?'

'I don't know,' said Zan, the sadness, the anxiety, in Jade's voice making his throat constrict.

Jade stopped. Her eyes were screwed up, her forehead creased, as if the effort of trying to squeeze out the memories was hurting.

'Where would your dad have been?' Zan found himself saying. 'Did he work?'

'That's it!' said Jade. 'That's where I went, to the factory. He was a foreman, at the factory!'

How did she know that? How could she sound so sure? Where did these ideas, these false memories come from? Was he encouraging them, prompting them with his questions? What the hell was he supposed to do?

'I thought I could see him,' she was saying, 'in his break. But I missed him. Break was already over when I got there. So I set off home to tell Mum. I was so excited, so keyed up, I wasn't concentrating and then I saw it! It was right in front of me. There was nothing I could do!'

8

'What?' said Zan. 'What was in front of you?'

'The lorry!' screamed Jade, turning round and round in circles on the pavement.

She was turning faster than she'd done out on the road. So fast she was almost spinning, making Zan dizzy watching.

'That's it, isn't it?' she said mid-spin. 'None of this is real, is it? It hit me, the lorry hit my bike. I never got home. I never got to tell them. I'm dead, aren't I? This isn't real. This is some sort of afterlife, some sort of test, some sort of hell.'

'O my God,' said Zan, grabbing her shoulders, trying to keep her still, as the first large spots of rain started to fall. 'You can feel that, can't you?' he said, squeezing a little tighter. 'How can you be dead? You can feel things, touch things!'

'Maybe I'm not dead,' she said with sudden hope. 'Maybe I'm just unconscious, in a coma or something.

I could wake up, if I tried, if I tried hard.'

'Jade,' Zan said, trying to get her moving forward again, 'it's not like that, is it? People don't live whole new lives when they're in coma. That sort of stuff only happens on TV or in stories.'

'How do you know?' she said.

Good question! He didn't know really. He didn't know anything about what happened in coma but he knew one thing for certain.

'Well, *I'm* real,' he said, 'not just something nasty lurking in your imagination!'

'You're just saying that! You're the one who's keeping me here, trapping me inside my head. Why can't you help me, help me to get back? I'm in the wrong body, Zan. The wrong time! I'm not supposed to be here. I don't want to be here.'

Her voice was getting sharper, more hysterical. Zan stopped steering her forward and got his mobile out. He had been going to wait until they got home but changed his mind. He needed to phone Mum now. He just couldn't handle this.

'This is all imagination,' Jade was saying, firmly, definitely. 'Nothing's real. I can do anything I like. Nothing can hurt me.'

She suddenly lunged towards the road, like she was drunk. Zan dropped his phone, which slid out in front of a car. There was a sharp crack as a car drove over

111

it. But it didn't matter. It was only a phone. At least he'd managed to grab Jade. It wasn't far now. If he could just keep hold of her, get her home, he could phone from there.

Zan left Jade in the kitchen while he went out into the hall to phone Mum. He left the door open so he could hear what she was doing, just in case she tried to escape. Escape! Shit, he was starting to think of her like she was some sort of loony. She wasn't, she was Jade, his sister. She was going to get through this. Whether it was the trauma, the tablets, both or neither, she was going to get better. He had to keep believing that.

He could hear her moving about as he made his call. She was opening and closing cupboards, like she was looking for something, a drink probably. If she'd slipped right back to being Janet, she'd have forgotten where everything was, wouldn't she? 'Slipped right back', the words lodged in his mind, sat there while he phoned Mum, as if they had some meaning, as if they were trying to tell him something. He didn't have time to think about it, he didn't want to leave Jade alone too long.

When he went back to the kitchen she was sitting at the table. She had a glass of water in front of her but she wasn't drinking it, she was fiddling in her bag, before fastening it up, hooking it over her shoulder.

'It was going to be so good,' she said. 'It was all working out right. He might even have let me go to university. I had two more years to work on him. That's what I was thinking when it happened, when I had the accident.'

This was worse than before, worse than that first day when she'd woken up claiming to be Janet. She was deeper into it, Zan could tell.

'But you can do all that,' he said, trying to connect on her level. 'You can do it as Jade, no probs! Dad's got a Uni fund set up for all of us and you can have my share as well, 'cos I'm not going. You could stay on forever, if that's what you want. Do a Master's, if you like, anything!'

She stared at him but didn't answer.

'I mean, if that's *all* you want,' he said, 'to go to sixth form and Uni, you're better off being Jade, aren't you?'

'No!' she said. 'I'm not Jade. I don't want to be Jade. I want to go back. I want to wake up. It's where I belong. I was happy there.'

'You were happy here, Jade,' he said, quietly.

It was true. Jade had always been the most easygoing, the most cheerful of the four of them. Claire was sort of intense, nervy. Gemma could be stroppy, cynical; nothing was ever quite right for her. He was happy enough, he supposed, when teachers and his parents left him alone, which mainly they didn't. But Jade, he'd never thought about it much before but Jade was very much like Mum: positive, optimistic, always able to make the best of things, until recently, until the night of the barbecue. Because you couldn't make the best of that, could you? Jade had tried, she'd definitely tried.

'I'm going to move on,' she'd said, the day she came out of hospital. 'I'm gonna get past it. I'll cope. I'm not gonna think about it ever again. I won't let him ruin my life.'

But he had. He'd ruined all their lives. Jade had endless flashbacks, nightmares, even before Janet appeared. She'd lost all her confidence, was scared to go out. And all the time, the tablets that were supposed to help were screwing her up, making it worse. They'd done it all wrong! They should have insisted on therapy right from the beginning, insisted she saw a counsellor instead of filling her up with pills. They should never have let her bury it all away. But they hadn't known, had they, just how bad it was going to get. Might the tablets have done permanent damage, could Jade's personality have split totally, irreversibly?

'I'm tired,' Jade said. 'I need to lie down.'

'I'll get you a blanket for the settee,' Zan said.

It would be safer in the lounge than upstairs. He could watch her more easily in there, until Mum got home.

Why wouldn't they go away? She was lying on the settee with her eyes closed but she could hear them whispering, sense them moving around; Jade's parents, Zan, the doctor, all muttering and staring at her. She could feel them staring. Why wouldn't they go, why wouldn't they leave her alone?

'*Leave me alone, leave me alone, leave me alone.*'

She could hear someone intoning those words but she knew it wasn't quite real, it couldn't be real. She wouldn't let it be real. The words were loud but hazy, echoing as if her mind was a huge, dark cave. And at the back of the cave, a small figure was cowering.

'*Don't touch me, don't do that, leave me alone.*'

Jade. It was Jade, yelling at someone, a man, a dark-haired man. No! She didn't want to know, didn't care. Jade wasn't real. Make her stop. Make her go away. She pictured the fog coming down, swirling round the cave. She pictured Jade shrinking, getting smaller and smaller and smaller until she wasn't there at all. Pictured herself growing, expanding, filling the space that Jade had left, battling as they'd done before. Only this time she was going to win. This time Jade wasn't coming back.

'I think she's asleep,' she heard someone say.

She concentrated on her breathing, making it heavy, rhythmic, feigning sleep until she heard them all leave the room. Good, that was what she wanted. It was time, time to kill off Jade completely, time to go home.

*

115

'Why?' Dad snapped at the doctor as soon as they got out into the hall. 'Why can't she go now?'

'I'm sorry,' Dr Carr said. 'I've told you. There aren't any beds at the moment but as soon as one becomes available I'll get her in.'

'And when might that be?' said Dad. 'Tomorrow, next week, next bloody month when it's too bloody late. Haven't you done enough bloody damage?'

'We're probably talking hours not days,' said Dr Carr. 'They're trying to sort out a bed for her. She's settled for the moment. It's not an emergency.'

'It is to me!' said Dad. 'This is my daughter we're talking about. Or at least it was until you screwed up with your bloody medication.'

'Doug,' Mum said, touching his arm.

He shrugged her off.

'What if we go private?' said Dad. 'Can we get her into a private ward?'

'I expect so,' said Dr Carr, 'but I don't think it's necessary. Look, let me try the hospital again before we decide.'

He went outside, probably more to get away from Dad than to make his call in private. Zan followed his parents into the kitchen, sat down next to Mum while Dad paced.

'What are they going to do, when they get her to hospital?' Zan asked.

'I'm not sure,' Mum said, 'but they can monitor things better, can't they? Maybe set up some intensive therapy. Change the medication again. I don't know. I thought the Janet business was over. I thought it had sorted itself out. But the stuff she's been saying. It's worse than ever.'

Zan looked at Dad, still pacing, glanced at the doctor standing out in the rain, making his calls. It probably wasn't the right time to mention his idea but it was better than the silence that had followed Mum's last statement.

'I was thinking,' Zan whispered, 'about her turning into Janet again. I mean, what if it's not a fantasy exactly?'

'Of course it's fantasy,' Mum said, attracting Dad's attention.

Zan paused. He didn't really want to share this with Dad but he had to tell someone before it drove him crazy.

'But what if it's not?' he persisted.

The phrase that had stuck in his mind earlier came back to him, 'slipped right back'.

'What if it's more like memories?' he said. 'A sort of regression, a past life or something that the tablets have somehow brought out, brought right to the front of Jade's mind.'

'What?' Dad snapped.

'It's just that it's all so detailed,' Zan pressed on, 'so real to her. The names, the exam grades, the colour of her school uniform. It can't all be made up. It must be coming from somewhere!'

'Imagination, she's always had a good imagination,' Mum said, wearily. 'That's why it's so detailed. She used to make up whole worlds with her toys when she was little. Then did the same sort of thing with that computer simulation thing she was obsessed with for a while. The detail's not the issue, Zan.'

'It's just,' said Zan, 'that, well, she was talking about possession the other day, like Janet was some sort of ghost, someone who really existed. And the school she talks about's real or at least it might be. I checked it out online.'

'Oh, for goodness sake!' said Dad, turning to face him. 'Ghosts! Don't you think things are bad enough without you behaving like a total prat, making them worse?'

Yeah, like Dad wasn't making things worse with his ranting, shouting and swearing!

'I'm sorry,' Zan said to Mum as Dad stormed out, probably to harass the doctor again. 'I just thought it was possible. Then when Jade started talking about the bike accident—'

'What bike accident?'

'At the school, when she freaked, she said she remembered being on her bike, being killed on her way home and I thought, I mean, it seemed like she might have slipped right back in her own mind to a time before she was even born. Maybe the tablets made her do that and . . . '

'Hey!' said Mum. 'Slow down.'

Zan took a deep breath. He knew he was doing it all wrong, talking too fast, spewing out all the random ideas that had been building up for days, weeks, leading him to do the stupid stuff he'd been doing online. Or maybe it wasn't so stupid.

'Past life memories,' he said, more slowly. 'People get them, don't they?'

'Not really, Zan, no,' Mum said, as if she was talking to a complete idiot. 'They might think they do but as far as I know there hasn't been a single case that stands up to any sort of scrutiny. And, besides, it's usually young kids, toddlers who start gibbering about other times, other places. Probably stuff they've seen on TV.'

'Not always,' said Zan. 'Grown-ups can remember stuff, I checked it out.'

'Only under therapy or hypnosis, though, isn't it?' said Mum. 'And even then it's memories implanted by the therapist, they reckon. It's all discredited mumbo-jumbo, Zan, and it's got nothing, absolutely nothing to do with what's going on with Jade.'

'Yeah, you're probably right,' said Zan. 'It's just that some of it seemed to fit. Like the way she's always been

119

freaky with bikes. I mean, if she'd been killed on a bike, in a previous life . . . '

'Zan,' Mum said, 'don't you see? You're getting it completely the wrong way round. Jade's never liked bikes so she makes up a bike accident for this Janet. Jade was struggling with her work, struggling to focus, knowing she couldn't possibly do her best, so she makes up super-good results for Janet. And the whole lot's made vivid because of the drugs and the stress. That's why it's so real to her!'

Outside the kitchen window Dad was waving his arms about, probably bombarding Dr Carr with questions while poor Dr Carr was still trying to make his call to the hospital. Neither of them seemed to notice the rain, which was getting heavier.

'Zan, are you OK?' Mum was asking. 'You've gone very pale.'

'Headache,' said Zan, rubbing his eyes.

The room felt heavy, oppressive, as if there was a storm building.

'I'll get you a paracetamol, then I'll go and check on Jade,' said Mum, getting up, opening a cupboard, standing for a moment, staring at it.

'Zan,' she began, 'have you moved the tablets?'

He stood up, knowing even before Mum spoke again.

'They've all gone, Jade's medication, everything. Some of the boxes are here but they're empty.'

120

That's what Jade had been doing earlier when she'd been opening and closing cupboards. She hadn't been looking for a drink, she'd been looking for tablets, stuffing them into her bag, probably. The bag she'd taken with her into the lounge.

Zan ran out of the kitchen. How could they have been so stupid, how could they have left her alone even for a second? With the state she was in, the warnings about those antidepressants. People had tried to harm themselves, tried to kill themselves. But not Jade. Oh God, not Jade, not that.

She wouldn't have had time. She couldn't have done it earlier. He'd been with her until the doctor turned up. And she'd been asleep when they left her, hadn't she? Besides they'd only been out of the lounge five minutes. Or was it longer? Oh God, it was longer! They must have been out of there for at least twenty minutes.

Mum had caught up with him by the time he reached the lounge and they pushed through the door together. Jade was slumped, half hanging off the settee, her right arm dangling, touching the floor. Her bag was open, bits of foil and empty tablet strips scattered around.

'Get Dr Carr,' Mum ordered, rushing forward, kneeling beside Jade. 'Phone an ambulance.'

Zan rushed back to the kitchen, banged on the window, shouted to Dr Carr then raced to the phone but all the time he was rushing around, it felt as though

121

life had gone into slow motion, as though it was taking half an hour to take every step, to lift the receiver. His fingers wouldn't work, wouldn't connect with the right numbers. There was no feeling in them. He kept hitting the wrong thing, having to start over. And all the time Jade was lying there unconscious or worse. Was it worse than that? Was it already too late?

9

'Janet? We're still here, love, we come everyday, your dad and me. Your friends come too sometimes and your sisters. We won't stop, none of us. No matter how long it takes, we won't ever stop. I know you'll come back to us, Janet. You're a fighter. You won't give up.'

'It's no good, Cath. She can't hear us.'

Yes, I can! But I can't answer. I'm lost, I'm trapped. I'm somewhere – different. But this is good, isn't it? I was right. I'm Janet. I had an accident. I'm in a coma, in hospital, where I've been all the time. This other girl, this other place, is just in my mind. All I have to do is break free. There was no Jade, no scars, no big house, no Zan. I made it up! I made it all up.

'We love you, Janet. You know that, don't you? We all love you so much.'

'Leave it, Cath. Come away now for a bit. Look at you! You need to rest.'

'We both do, Joe. But how can we? I lie awake at

night, trying to bargain with a God I'm not sure I believe in anymore, begging him to let her come back to us, telling him I'll do anything, give anything, give up my own life willingly, as long as he doesn't take Janet.'

'I know, Cath, I know.'

'But he's not listening. Why isn't he listening?'

'He might be. We don't know, do we? There might still be a chance.'

'It's almost six weeks now. And every day, I think that maybe today . . .'

'Come on, Cath. We really have to go now. Sister's staring at us! Visiting time finished over an hour back. I'm surprised she's let us stay so long.'

'All right, in a minute, just let me say goodnight to her.'

No! Mum, don't go. I can hear you. I'm here. I can hear you. I'm coming back. Don't go. Not now. Don't leave me.

'Goodnight, pet. We'll see you tomorrow. Maybe you'll be awake, then eh? Come back to us, Janet. Please. Just come back.'

'I'm trying! I'm almost there.'

'Don't move, don't scream or you're dead!'

'No! Go away, leave me alone. You don't belong here. I won't let you in. I'm not listening to you. I'm listening to them. You can't touch me. You're not real. Jade's not real.'

'That's it, Jade. Come on. I need you to be awake for

124

a minute. Good girl. I know this feels bad but we're going to help you, OK?'

Who are you? Go away. Go away! You're killing her, you're killing Janet. You're killing the wrong one!

It was still raining when Zan and his dad left the hospital. Heavy rain, torrential, blowing in their faces, bouncing up at them from the ground but Zan barely felt it. His body was too numb, too cold already to notice. He hadn't really wanted to leave but Mum had said it was best. There was nothing they could do. She'd phone if there was any change. So he'd been despatched with Dad to pick up Claire from the station.

Zan glanced at the clock as they got in the car. It was almost midnight. The train was due in ten minutes. They should just be in time. Claire had insisted on coming home all the way from Brighton, where she was supposed to be on a training course. Gemma too was trying to change her flight, come back tomorrow instead of next week. Both of them had totally freaked; Claire crying down the phone, Gemma barely able to speak. It was worse for them, in a way. They hadn't expected it, had they? They'd thought Jade was making progress. Mum and Dad still hadn't told them much about the Janet business. And, OK, they'd mentioned the dodgy antidepressants to Claire, but not how much damage they'd caused. They'd done it for the best. They

125

hadn't seen the point in worrying Claire and Gemma. But it was wrong; another wrong choice, another wrong decision.

Zan watched the windscreen wipers furiously swishing away the rain as Dad drove in silence, looking in his mirror, pulling into the side of the road as they heard sirens and two fire engines zipped past. They hadn't got much further when they heard more sirens and had to move over for an ambulance, followed closely by two police cars. There was obviously a major crisis somewhere, a motorway crash maybe. More lives ripped apart in an instant.

The delay meant they were a bit late at the station. Claire was outside waiting for them, huddled under the overhanging roof to keep dry. Her face looked drawn, yellowish almost, but perhaps that was just the lights. She darted over to the car, slinging her bag onto the back seat, clambering in.

'How is she?' Claire asked, before she'd even closed the door.

'Stable,' Dad said, repeating what they'd been told before they left. 'Mercifully we knew more or less what she'd taken so they could act pretty quickly, give her something to neutralise the drugs, get her stomach pumped out. They've got her on a drip now and they're doing blood tests and stuff.'

It sounded bland, matter of fact, barely reflecting

what had really gone on during the day. Following the ambulance in Dad's car, the pacing, the waiting, the endless questions, forms to be filled in, trying to co-operate, trying to think, trying to keep calm, battling the fear that Jade might not make it, might not pull through. Hours and hours of waiting, feeling useless, wanting to do something, knowing there was nothing left.

'Can I see her,' asked Claire, 'now, tonight?'

'It's best not,' said Dad. 'She's conscious now but she needs to rest.'

'And so do you by the sound of it,' said Claire, quietly.

'We'll go tomorrow, first thing,' said Dad. 'Your mum's with her, she'll be all right,' he added as if desperately trying to convince himself.

'So what have they said about the long term?' Claire asked.

Zan turned round, taking over, answering the dozens of questions that followed so that Dad could concentrate on his driving, on getting through the flooding that seemed to have sprung up everywhere. They'd have more idea about the long-term prospects, doctors had said, once they got the test results back, once they knew whether there'd been any damage to the vital organs. It was unlikely, they thought, because the drugs hadn't been in her system for long. There'd be psychiatric assessments too, which was usual in the case of attempted suicide.

Claire flinched as he said the word.

'I don't think she was trying to do that,' Zan said. 'She didn't want to die. She was confused, wouldn't have known what she was doing.'

Claire listened, shaking her head, playing with her rings, twisting them round and round on her fingers as he tried to explain about Janet. But how could he when he barely understood it himself? The strength of it, the power it had over Jade. He'd almost started to believe in Janet himself, believe that she was, in some way, real. Almost, who was he kidding? He did believe in Janet. But he didn't tell Claire that.

Back at the house Claire fussed around Dad, insisting on making tea and toast even though he said he couldn't eat anything. He managed half the drink before going off to bed, though Zan doubted that he'd sleep. Zan ate the toast, feeling guilty that he was hungry, that he could even think about food.

He didn't think he'd manage to sleep but as soon as he lay down total exhaustion kicked in and it seemed barely five minutes until Claire was shouting him. It was only half past seven but they'd agreed to get up early; there was stuff to do, people to contact, arrangements to make before they could set off.

'Check out the email, Zan,' Dad said, when they'd had breakfast. 'Gemma's supposed to be sending her flight and train details. Print it out for me, eh? I think I'll ring the hospital.'

'I thought Mum was going to phone us about half eight?' Claire said.

'She is,' he said, sharply. 'But I need to check now.'

Zan left Claire clearing up and switched on the computer. Gemma's mail was there. She'd be back by late afternoon. He let his eyes scan the other mails while he switched the printer on. There were messages from Friends Reunited. Did he have time to look, did he want to look? Maybe he should just do Gemma's printout, focus on what was important.

But the Janet thing was important, wasn't it? He needed to know if only to wipe out the crazy ideas that had been niggling at him. There were two messages. They'd both replied! As Gemma's details printed out, Zan looked at first one message, then the other, barely able to take in what he was seeing.

'Zan, what the hell's that?'

Zan instinctively clicked the window shut.

'Let me see that,' Dad said.

Zan reluctantly opened it, sensed Dad peering over his shoulder reading Lydia Bayley's curt message basically accusing Zan of being a sick nutter and telling him to stop pestering her with questions about her family.

'Bloody hell, Zan!' Dad said. 'I don't believe this. You've been harassing this woman about…about Janet, just because her name's Bayley? Have you tracked down every bloody Bayley on the net?'

'No!' said Zan. 'I told you yesterday – I was looking at this school and I just wanted to check. I didn't mention the details or give my name or nothing, I just asked...'

Dad grabbed the top of the chair, swung it round so that Zan was facing him. Dad's face was red, his eyes screwed up almost as if he was in physical pain.

'It doesn't matter what you asked,' Dad yelled. 'Jade almost died! And you're mucking about pestering total bloody strangers. What bloody planet are you on, Zan? Jade's not possessed by some dead girl from years back. She's not a bloody reincarnation! She's screwed up by the pills and what that bloody bastard did to her. She might never get better!'

Zan pushed back in his chair as Dad's fists clenched, certain his dad was going to hit him. Dad, who'd never hit anyone! The chair crashed into the desk, Dad's fists unclenched, his expression changed from fury to – what? It was hard to read. Almost as though there was no expression there at all. Utter blankness. Hopelessness.

'Oh God, I'm sorry,' Dad said, stepping back, out of Zan's personal space. 'But this is madness, Zan. Janet isn't real, hasn't ever been real.'

He paused, rubbing at his forehead.

'I guess we've all gone a bit crazy,' he said. 'I don't know what's happening. I can almost...almost feel how it must be for Jade,' he added quietly. 'Sometimes, I just don't recognise myself anymore.'

He moved as if to leave. Zan picked up the printout, handed it to him.

'Flight's due in at midday,' Zan said, trying to keep his voice steady. 'If Gem can get the two-fifteen train she should be at the station by half four.'

Dad nodded, took the piece of paper, put it in his pocket without looking at it.

'Can you pack up?' he said. 'I want to get going in five minutes.'

'What did the hospital say? When you phoned?'

'Not much but I spoke to your mum as well. Jade had a bad night but they reckon she's out of danger...physically, at least. Hopefully the first of the test results should be through by the time we get there. So hurry up, OK?'

Zan turned off the printer but not the computer. Despite what Dad had said, he needed to look one more time. Not at Lydia's message but at the other one. The one Dad hadn't seen; the one from Susan Bayley. It was just as short, just as snappy in a way as Lydia's, but a bit more informative. He looked, committing it to memory, as he shut everything down. It was totally weird, bizarre. Not what he'd expected at all.

He wasn't sure what he'd expected but it wasn't that. He stood up as the computer finished shutting down but he didn't move straight away. He needed a minute on his own to think it out. Think if it could possibly mean anything. It had to! It couldn't be coincidence. He half closed his eyes, seeing the message:

I'm not sure who you are and I don't want you contacting me again. But I'll answer your questions. Yes, my sister, Janet, had a bad accident in her teens but no, she's most certainly not dead.

That was weird enough, the connection, the accident. But Janet wasn't dead. He'd been totally wrong. It wasn't a past life Jade had been living. Of course it wasn't. Mum was right. It was a crazy idea, completely mad. But then Susan's message, this new possibility, was crazy too. Not so much the first bit but the last bit. It was the last bit that had really freaked him. *No, she's most certainly not dead. She's alive & well & living in*... their town! The Janet he'd tracked down would be what, in her fifties or sixties? And she was living somewhere near them!

'Zan, are you ready?'

He moved out of the sitting room, heading towards the kitchen. OK, so there was a real Janet, who'd once had a bad accident and was now living in their town. So might Jade somehow know her? Could this Janet have once told Jade her story? That had to be it, didn't it?

Then could the trauma, the tablets, have twisted the story in Jade's mind into some sort of reality? Why though, out of all the stories Jade must have read or heard over the years, why pick that one? Or maybe she hadn't chosen it. Maybe it wasn't as logical as that. Like dreaming, you didn't choose what to dream, did you? It just happened.

Claire handed him his jacket. He took it, put it on, while Dad was obsessively checking that the windows were all shut, all the switches turned off. No way could Zan tell anyone what he'd found. Not Mum, not Claire, not anybody. He couldn't risk Dad finding out, kicking off at him again.

So what to do? Was it important, did it matter? Did it make any difference to anything? Ought he to push harder to find the real Janet Bayley, to find out where she was living? Would it help Jade to know where it was all coming from? To know there was some sort of logic, some sort of explanation? If she could understand that it wasn't ghosts or some freaky past life, would it help her to get better?

The phone ringing jolted him back to the present. Jade. It might be the hospital. Dad was already out in the hall, picking it up. Zan and Claire both hovered by the door, listening but it was impossible to make anything out from Dad's short replies of 'oh', 'right', 'I see' and 'yes'. Then there was a sudden change of tone that drew both Claire and Zan out into the hall.

'Why?' Dad was saying. 'I don't get it. Are you sure? O my God! Did she? Has she? Yes, yes, I understand.'

Dad stood, silently listening, nodding at the phone for a few minutes longer before muttering goodbye and putting it down.

'Was that the hospital?' Claire asked.

'No,' said Dad, 'no, it was the police.'

'Police, why?' said Zan. 'What's happened?'

'Have they picked him up?' said Claire.

'No,' said Dad, again, as if he was still trying to process something, work it out. 'Not yet but . . . it's a bit complex, come on, let's get going, I'll tell you in the car.'

Claire sat in the front with Dad so Zan leant forward, arms resting on the back of the passenger seat, straining to listen. Not that there was anything to listen to at first. Dad waited until he'd reversed out of the drive before he began.

'The fire engines, the ambulance we saw last night, Zan,' he said. 'They were on their way to a house fire – at the Mellors'.'

'Was it deliberate?' said Zan. 'Was it arson?'

'The police think so because of the other stuff but they won't know for certain until they've done all the checks. The inside of the house was gutted apparently – completely burnt out.'

'Was anyone inside? Were any of them hurt?'

Zan was surprised to hear himself asking the questions, even more surprised to realise that part of him cared.

10

'Smoke inhalation, mostly,' Dad said, 'but two of the lads are pretty badly burnt – Ricky and one of the younger ones.'

'Davy?'

'No, I don't think so. Can't remember,' he said as though it didn't much matter which of them had been hurt, or how seriously. 'Anyway the younger lad was trapped inside, apparently. Ricky went back for him, managed to drag him out.'

Ricky with all his bullying, all his aggro, had gone back into a burning building for his brother. That took guts. Zan wondered whether he'd have been brave enough to do the same for Claire or Gemma or Jade.

'Quite the bloody hero,' Dad added.

The coldness, the venom, in Dad's voice was scarier even than the clenched fists and swearing earlier. He didn't seem to care that a kid had almost burnt to death, as if he couldn't see past his own hurt, Jade's hurt, like he had no other emotions left.

'They're not in the same hospital as Jade, thank God,' Dad was saying. 'The police are moving them all out of the area to a safe house.'

'Can't understand why they didn't do it earlier,' Claire said.

'They tried but the Mellors refused to move,' said Dad, dismissively before adding, 'Said they had nothing to be ashamed of and all that crap. Anyway, there's something else, something important. Mrs Mellor's given the police a lead. She's finally told them where she thinks her brother might be.'

'Why?' said Claire. 'Why now? Was it some sort of deal, police protection in return for information? Or were they just scared by this last attack?'

'Neither,' said Dad, braking sharply at the lights. 'What made her change her mind was the girl who was stabbed to death in a park in Nottingham on Thursday.'

'I saw that,' said Zan, 'on the news! O my God, is that where she thinks he is, in Nottingham?'

'Police didn't really give me any details,' said Dad, pulling away from the lights. 'But yes, Mrs Mellor's pretty sure. The girl was fourteen. Fourteen,' Dad repeated, his voice suddenly hoarse.

Zan had been wrong. Dad did have emotions, sympathy, left but it was selective.

'I mean, they had to bloody wait, didn't they?' Dad

said, his voice still raspy, uneven. 'They've known all along where he was hiding out but they had to bloody wait until he killed someone.'

'It's not certain it was him, though,' said Claire.

Claire was right. It wasn't certain, nothing had been proved. But the Mellors obviously thought so. It had shocked them into action. Their loyalty, their blindness, their denial, it seemed, had limits.

Jade was awake when they arrived but Mum said it was best if she didn't have too many visitors at once. Zan let Claire go in with Dad while he went to the café with Mum so she could have a cup of tea; the first thing she'd drunk or eaten since Jade was admitted yesterday.

'I don't know whether she'll talk to them,' Mum said, on the way to the café. 'She hasn't said much at all. It's like she's back to where she was between the exams finishing and Janet surfacing. Saying more in her sleep than she does when she's awake, crying sometimes.'

The doctors had warned them right from the start, right from the day it happened, that it could take a long time, years sometimes, for people to recover from something like that. A violent sexual assault. Zan shuddered. He'd finally said the words, at least in his own mind. Violent sexual assault. Not a rape. Jade had, somehow, managed to fight him off. Where did people find the almost supernatural strength, the courage, to do something like that?

Fight off a guy holding a knife, run back into a burning building to rescue your kid brother. Adrenalin, one of the doctors had once told him, the fight or flight mechanism.

'So we don't know if she's remembered anything?' Zan asked, as they joined the short queue in the café.

Mum shook her head.

'Hard to say but I don't think so, not really. She's tearful. I think maybe the memories are starting to come back but she's fighting them. I just don't know,' Mum said, sighing as she sat down with her drink.

Zan told her about the fire, the Mellors, Nottingham, Dad's reaction. Though he didn't mention Dad's earlier anger and what had caused it. Mum was finding it hard enough to cope with facts let alone freaky coincidences that might or might not be important.

After sipping her drink, Mum said she needed some fresh air, so they went for a walk round the hospital grounds and when they got back to Jade's room she was asleep again. Claire had brought a nightdress for her instead of the hospital gown. One of the ones with long sleeves that hid the scars, the marks where he'd slashed at her, marks that would fade in time – maybe quicker than the mental scars.

Jade stayed asleep for most of the day, waking only when the nurses woke her for her medication, saying little before dozing off again so it was impossible to tell if she was Jade or Janet or whether there was anything going on inside her head at all. Later, when Dad went to pick up Gemma, Claire went with him, not trusting him to be alone. Zan stayed with Mum taking turns watching Jade until a nurse came to tell Mum that the doctor would like a word with her.

Zan moved away from the window, where he'd been staring at nothing in particular, and went to sit on the chair next to Jade's bed. She was moaning slightly, eyelids flickering. Dreaming, she was dreaming again. Suddenly her eyes snapped open and she sat up in one fluid movement with no warning. Her back was straight, her arms stretched out.

'Janet's dead,' she murmured. 'She's left me, they've all left me.'

She wasn't awake. She might be sitting up, she might be talking, but she wasn't awake.

'No,' Zan said, hoping his words might somehow get through. 'No, Janet isn't dead. She didn't die, Jade. Janet's fine and you will be too.'

He stretched out, held her hand and pressed it slightly, trying to calm her, wondering whether he should press the emergency buzzer, call a nurse.

'Zan?' Jade said.

Her eyes weren't seeing him. It was his voice, his voice she was responding to or the pressure of his hand maybe.

'Yeah,' he said quietly. 'It's me. You're OK. Lie down, eh?'

She flopped back, resting against the pillows again, her eyes closing. She'd responded to his instruction, she must he able to hear him.

'*She didn't die, Jade. Janet didn't die.*'

'*I did! She did. You're lying. You're just saying that, trying to trick me.*'

'*You're OK, Jade. You're gonna be all right.*'

'*Go away. Get out of my dream. Leave me alone.*'

'*There's no ghost, no Janet, there's only you in there, Jade.*'

'*And him. He's here too. He's hurting her, he's hurting Jade. I don't want to see. He's hurting her. He won't stop. He won't stop.*'

'*Jade, can you still hear me? You'll get through this. I know you will. You have to.*'

'*You're not listening to me! I can't. I can't let him do that. I can't be Jade. I can't let him back. I'm not Jade. I don't want to be Jade. I don't want to see. It's not happening. Leave me alone. Help me. Mum! Help me. Stop him. Please.*'

Zan gently let go of her hand. There was no point talking to her anymore. She was back in deep sleep, she couldn't hear him. Maybe she hadn't really heard any of it. Not that it would have done any good if she had.

Her head was shaking from side to side now, as if she

140

was trying to shake something off. Where was she? What was happening in her mind?

Knife, at her throat, point pressing under her chin, forcing her back into the alleyway. Other hand grabbing her hair, yanking her head back, scalp ripping, burning. She shouldn't have stopped. Hadn't been thinking. Was angry. Thinking about something else. Hadn't been careful. Own stupid fault. Shouldn't have stopped. Should have run. His body, heavy, pushing against her. Hard lips pressing down on hers, sucking, nibbling, biting, his breath stale, poisonous, his tongue slimy. Her stomach retching, scalp still burning. Pain, too much pain. Hard to breathe. Choking back sobs. Quiet, keep quiet. Tears, sweat, mingling. Face wet, dripping. His mouth by her ear now. Whispering, threatening. Threatening to kill. To cut her face. Don't listen. Don't listen to him. Knife sliding down her neck, onto her chest, tearing through her shirt, grazing her skin. Hand releasing her hair, moving down, touching her, tugging her clothes, groping under her skirt. Rough skin, sharp nails digging into her thigh. Fingers crawling, mauling. Tip of the knife pressing into her side. Right side, beneath her ribs. Pressing deeper. Knife, hands, nails, mouth. Leave me alone. Leave me alone. Please. Stop. Got to make him stop. Don't think about what he's doing. Not happening. Not happening. Don't freeze, don't think about the pain. Don't think. Do something. Do something. Stop him. Voices. Someone coming. Someone there, out on the street. Someone to help me. Now. Do it now. Push, kick. Knife slashing. Keep kicking, pushing, thumping. Knife clattering on the floor, hand sharp across her face, head smashed back against the wall. No pain. Don't feel it. Run. Now. While he's picking up the knife. Scream. Run. Help me, someone help me.

'Help me!'

Zan's finger went to the buzzer as Jade cried out but he didn't need to press it. Her scream had brought nurses running. Within minutes the doctor was there and Mum, pushing Zan out of the way, holding Jade who was crying now like she'd done that evening when those people had brought her home, crying on and on as if she'd never stop. And there was nothing he could do except stand there, leaning against the white-painted wall, listening to her cry, recognising it, knowing that the memories were back.

More doctors and nurses going in and out with drinking water, tablets; changing the drip, talking to Mum, talking to Jade. At some point, though Zan barely knew when, Dad came back with Claire and Gemma. A psychologist arrived; not Dr Mitchell, someone else. He and his sisters were gently herded out. Not knowing where to go, what to do, they ended up sitting on a low wall outside the hospital, even though it was damp, chilly like summer had changed sometime during the past two days to winter without bothering with autumn.

He watched Claire lighting a cigarette, listened to Gemma moaning at her, telling her she was an idiot, she should quit.

'I had,' Claire snapped.

The three of them sat in silence for what seemed forever until Gemma spoke, words bursting out as if she'd suddenly remembered.

'Dad got a phone call,' she said, turning to look at Zan, 'just as we were leaving the station. They've arrested him.'

Him, it was weird that, how they never said his name. As if the name itself was cursed, evil, like you just couldn't speak it.

'He was in Nottingham,' Claire added, 'like Mrs Mellor said.'

It was important, massively important. The news they'd been waiting for, praying for. But Zan was finding it hard to focus, hard to listen, hard to see anything except Jade. Yet somehow, the words filtered through.

'He didn't go quietly,' Claire was saying. 'He jumped out of a window, apparently, straight through the glass, stabbed one of the cops, when they cornered him. Fortunately the guy was wearing protective clothing.'

'It means they've got enough to charge him with though,' Gemma added, 'at least for now. Even without Jade or the Nottingham murder.'

'Do you think it'll help?' said Claire.

'What?' Zan asked.

'Jade. Do you think it'll help her, knowing that they've got him?'

'It might,' Gemma said. 'But …'

She didn't finish, she didn't have to. They all knew what she meant. It would always be with Jade, with all of them. Whether he was in gaol, out of gaol, alive or dead, it couldn't change anything. For some other potential victim, maybe, but not for Jade.

'Hey, Zan!'

He looked up the road. Two girls were hurrying towards him, Hannah and Millie.

'We heard about Jade,' Millie said.

How? How did stuff get round so fast? Granted Hannah and Millie were the sort who knew everything two days before it happened but even so!

'Been trying to phone,' said Hannah.

'It's knackered,' said Zan. 'My phone's knackered. I've been using an old one of Mum's,' he said, getting it out of his pocket.

'Oh, right,' said Hannah. 'When we couldn't get through, Mum phoned the hospital but they wouldn't tell her much. How is she?'

Zan switched the phone on while Claire was answering Hannah. He wasn't expecting anything because he'd only given a couple of people the new number but they must have passed it on and word about Jade had definitely got round, way beyond Hannah and Millie. There were dozens of missed calls and texts from all sorts of people, even people he barely knew! One from Lewis – well he'd sort of expected that – but Woody, for heaven's sake and Lisa – which Lisa, who the hell was Lisa? Whoever they were, they were all asking questions, wishing Jade well. Wishing! If only. If only you could wave a magic wand, wish it all away, wish everything back to the way it was.

'Have you heard about Ricky Mellor?' he heard Millie say, as he replied to a couple of texts.

He wasn't really listening. Yeah, he knew about Ricky, knew about the fire. He didn't want to think about it but he had. All the time he'd been thinking, worrying about Jade, other images had butted in, images of the burning house, of Ricky and his brother lying in hospital, of bandages, drips, burns, skin grafts, scars. The pictures in his head were bad enough; he didn't need Millie to tell him the details, the gossip, the rumours. Except what Millie said next didn't sound like rumour. It sounded definite, horribly definite and final.

'He died,' she said. 'Ricky died, late this morning, in hospital.'

11

Jade sat down in the waiting room next to Gemma. The waiting room with its pastel colours, comfortable chairs and bright, reassuring posters. It was designed to be peaceful, relaxing. There was even a vase of fresh flowers on the small table and music, like the sound of the sea, rippling from hidden speakers.

None of it helped. She didn't want to be here but she didn't have a choice. It was part of the deal. They'd let her out of hospital on the Sunday, let her go home like she'd wanted, but she had to attend the clinic. Twice a week at first, gradually, hopefully, cutting down to once a week, once a fortnight, once a month until she no longer needed the support.

Now that she'd remembered, she had to talk, they said. Had to open up about *it*; the attack. The attack that had happened more than three months ago yet which felt like only three days. It was all back now with an intensity that almost choked her, made it difficult to move, difficult to breathe, difficult to sleep, even more difficult to wake up again and make herself get out of bed. His face, his voice were everywhere, the feel of him, the smell of him.

There'd been a time, in between, they'd told her, when she hadn't remembered it at all. She'd done exams, passed them even. How was that possible? Even freakier, she'd been living a sort of alternative life, lost in the back of her own mind like some sort of waking coma. Wherever it was she'd lost herself, she wished she could go back, be anywhere except here. But she couldn't, could she? That was someone else's life, not hers, a life she'd borrowed for a while. She knew that now, she was beginning to understand, piecing together things her parents had told her with bits from her own memory so it was slowly starting to make some sort of sense, but it was still scary. Scary to think that you could be lost, for weeks, months like that, inside your own head. Lost time that you couldn't ever get back.

It was largely down to the antidepressants, they'd virtually admitted. Nothing had been proved yet but there were too many cases for it to be coincidence. People in their teens and twenties mainly, who'd suffered hallucinations, developed suicidal tendencies. No one had used the S word in her case, at least not to her face. That's how they thought about it though, she was sure. But they were wrong. She'd never wanted to kill herself.

Somehow in the crazy mixed-up mess that was her mind, the overdose had been a way to stay alive.

There'd be compensation. The pharmaceutical company would probably settle out of court, for a *significant sum*, Dad's solicitor had stressed, to keep it as quiet as possible, minimise publicity. She could press for other compensation too – for the parole board messing up; releasing someone who should never have been released. Dad was keen to go for it. Like money could make any difference! Like you could buy back your old life or walk into a shop and demand a new one.

'I'd like a shiny new life please. I'd like to start over.'

Starting over, that's what it was all about, wasn't it? Learning to confront it, learning to face the fear. She could feel her limbs tense, felt Gemma's hand lightly touching her arm. Mum or Dad had come the first few times, now Gemma. Zan had volunteered but term had started today. Jade felt her body involuntarily twitch as the doctor's door opened. The doctor had her coat on – long, grey, stylish, expensive. They were going for a walk, like they'd done last time. Just her and the doctor; Gemma would stay. She was already pulling a thick book from her bag as Jade stood up.

Walking, outside. Such a simple thing, the sort of thing you took for granted. One foot in front of the other without your legs shaking, your eyes darting everywhere, wondering who was looking at you, what they were thinking. This was no random walk either. Last week they'd just had a stroll, been into a couple of shops. She'd repeated the exercise with Mum, with Zan. The daily walk, the challenge!

She'd done well, they'd said, so this week they were going to see someone. A girl called Aliss, who'd been attacked three years ago, by a gang, when she was fifteen. Aliss didn't know the gang; she hadn't done anything to provoke them. It was mindless, pointless and totally random. Aliss's nose had been broken and her left arm. Two ribs had been cracked when they'd kicked her, as she lay on the ground. The gang had filmed the attack on their phones, laughed as they did it. For months afterwards Aliss was sick whenever she heard someone laugh.

Aliss was doing well now, though, holding down a part-time job, going out with friends, hoping to start college soon. Aliss was a success story. Aliss would talk to her, show her it was possible. What would she be like, this Aliss, this girl who'd fought off the flashbacks, the nightmares, the sickness, the anger? This girl who hadn't tried to hide, who'd faced up to her experiences and moved on, this walking bloody miracle girl!

Jade felt her legs stop moving. She didn't want to go and 'share her story', telling it again and again and again and again until it slowly bled from her system. Dizziness swamped her and she clutched onto the doctor. The doctor half-turned, held her steady, waiting, smiling at her more with her calm, dark eyes than her lips. A smile that said You're doing OK, Jade. I'm proud of you. We're all proud of you.

Jade tried to breathe more deeply, like she'd been taught, forcing the oxygen into her blood, letting her limbs loosen. She took another step. She'd go and see Aliss. What choice did she have?

At lunchtime, Zan stood in the queue that snaked from the reception desk right back along the main corridor. He was waiting to collect work for Jade. She was going to have a home tutor for a while but the school was providing materials, making sure she didn't miss out, so that hopefully, she'd be able to come back – when she was ready.

He shuffled forward, wishing they'd hurry up. He didn't want to listen to the chatter going on around him, the buzz of gossip about Ricky and his uncle. Everyone knew about Ricky now, or at least all the seniors did; they'd been told in assembly. The Ricky who used to swear and chuck chairs at teachers became 'a lively boy who was never afraid to speak up for himself or challenge authority'. But that's how it was when someone died, wasn't it? You didn't say any of the bad stuff, didn't speak ill of the dead. You had to be really, really bad, like Hitler, for someone to diss you once you were dead. And Ricky wasn't all bad, was he?

They'd been told something else in assembly too, about the cause of the fire, about how it had been caused by some freak electrical fault. How there'd been no smoke alarms, so no one had realised until it was too late. It was an accident, not arson, not murder or manslaughter, not some misguided attempt at revenge for Jade. Did that make it any better? Maybe – but it didn't change the end result, did it?

Behind him he could hear a couple of girls, gibbering about Ricky's uncle, saying that the trial would be next week. He could have put them right but he couldn't be bothered. The trial wouldn't be for months yet! It took ages for all the paper work to crawl its way though the system.

'Bloody typical,' Dad had snarled. 'Just give the victims time to start recovering then haul them into bloody court to give evidence so it all kicks off all over again.'

The police had tried to reassure him, telling him Jade might not even go to court, not with all the other evidence they'd accumulated. They might be able to spare her that. Zan hoped so. It was going to be hard enough for Jade without all that hassle. He'd tried not to think about it too much but he couldn't help it. The questions just went on and on. Was the new therapy working? How long would it take? Was there ever a 'real' Janet? Would they ever find out?

He was near the front of the queue now. There were two people who Mrs Simmonds dealt with in her usual efficient way, then Woody, from his own year, taking for ever to sign his name in the detention book. How could anybody get a detention when they'd only been back three hours? Just as Woody scurried off, the office phone rang. Another delay! Zan's arms folded and unfolded themselves as he watched Mrs Simmonds move slowly towards the phone and pick it up. She wasn't using her stick today. It must be one of her better days.

He looked at her stick propped against the wall, glanced at her name in thick red letters on the office door, Mrs Janet Simmonds, and, as he looked from one to the other, an idea landed in his head, perfectly formed, perfectly clear. So clear that he wondered why he hadn't thought of it before. But in a way he had. It had been half there when Jade first started hallucinating. It had vaguely resurfaced when he'd got that weird email from Susan Bayley telling him that her sister, Janet, lived in their town, but there'd been so many other things going on, so many other things to stress about, it had sort of got pushed aside. But now it was back and it just seemed so obvious. Or was it? Was he just seeing what he wanted to see, desperate to find something that made some sort of sense?

'Right,' said Mrs Simmonds, glancing at him, as she

put the phone down. 'You've come for Jade's books. How is she?'

'She's doing OK,' said Zan, automatically giving the same response he'd given to everyone that day.

'Good,' said Mrs Simmonds, looking behind him at the rest of the queue, as she moved back towards the reception desk. 'I'll pop round and see her when she's up to it. Tell her I was asking though, won't you?'

She bent down, picked up a box and plonked it in front of him. Zan wanted to ask her about his theory, his idea, but how could he without sounding rude, personal, or even worse, mad? He opened his mouth but it was too late, she'd already started dealing with the two girls behind him and the bell was ringing so he picked up the box and headed to his form room.

Maybe he'd ask her some other time, or maybe he should just let it drop. He was probably wrong, anyway.

Jade woke up when Zan burst in. She uncurled from the armchair and stretched her legs as Zan dumped a box of books in front of her.

'So how did it go?' he said, flopping onto the floor next to the box. 'With Aliss?'

Typical of Zan, straight in there!

'She was great,' Jade said. 'I was dreading it but she was really – normal.'

153

Zan was nodding and it felt natural, easy, talking to him somehow, just like it had been with Aliss.

'I mean, I thought she was going to be dead brave or special but she reckons not. Said she went through all the stages I'm going through. The exhaustion, denial, paranoia, partial amnesia, everything. Maybe not so intense, because she didn't have the dodgy pills but more or less the same.'

'A normal reaction to an abnormal situation.'

'Uh?'

'Post-traumatic stress – something I read. Talking of which,' Zan said, pointing to the box of books, 'looks like you're gonna be busy! There's about a million books in there and a few more cards to add to your collection. Everyone's been asking about you. Hannah, Millie, Lewis, Mrs Prior, Mrs Simmonds.'

He emphasised the last name, paused for a moment, like he wanted to say something but wasn't quite sure.

'I had a thought about her today,' he eventually said, 'about all the time you spent with her during exams and about her bad leg and her name and everything.'

He paused again, shuffling, fidgeting.

'I know it sounds crazy,' he went on, talking faster this time, 'but I just thought maybe her bad leg was caused by an accident, way back. I thought she maybe told you about it. That she might somehow be *your* Janet, you know?' he added, uncertainly. 'Janet Bailey?'

'It's not crazy,' said Jade, half-smiling, not really surprised that Zan had worked it out. 'You're right. Bayley was her maiden name and, yeah, I think a lot of my hallucination stuff was based on her.'

'What?' said Zan. 'You mean you knew? You knew where it was coming from? You always knew?'

'No, not at the time,' said Jade. 'At the time, it was totally real, so real it just felt part of me. But I've been sort of unravelling it, thinking of stuff Mrs Simmonds talked about between exams. You know how she gibbers on! She was trying to keep me occupied, I guess, telling me about her childhood, her family and everything. I can't remember all of it. I don't think I was even taking it in properly at the time, not consciously anyway but I know she told me about her bike accident, about spending three months in a coma, then several years in a wheelchair. So, yeah, I guess it was her life I was replaying – or, at least parts of it.'

'Blimey!' said Zan. 'When did you work it out? Why didn't you tell us? Why didn't you say something?'

'I don't know. It sort of crept up bit by bit, in amongst all the other stuff. Then it finally clicked into place this morning, when I was waiting for my appointment. Like finishing a puzzle.'

'Blimey,' said Zan again, standing up, pacing around.

'I think,' said Jade, 'that I latched onto Mrs Simmonds' story because she was so upbeat, so positive about everything. She made her life sound good – even though it wasn't always. I'm not sure – I still don't quite know what my brain was up to but it's made me feel a bit better, knowing where most of it came from.'

'So d'you reckon all the detail was right,' Zan said, 'or did you make some of it up?'

'I don't know,' said Jade, stretching her arms, loosening her shoulders. 'I might talk to her about it, sometime. Or would that be too freaky? Anyway, come on, I think it's about time for my daily walk. We can talk and walk at the same time.'

'You sure you want to? You're not too tired?'

'No, I'm OK, I want to.'

She stood up, amazed to find that she meant it. One day, like Aliss, she'd be able to go to the place where it happened. One day she'd be able to go out alone, talk about it without crying; get by without any medication at all.

'Come on then,' said Zan. 'We'll walk as far as the bridge and back, eh? Or even pop in and see Hannah, if you're up to it.'

Jade smiled as she followed him out. She was doing it. Step by step, she was doing it. There was nowhere to hide anymore; no fog, no Janet, no borrowed life, no going back.

Forward was the only way she had left.